This is Bob Cattell's second book of short stories set in cricket-playing countries around the world. It follows his *First XI*, published in 2015.

The stories in this collection are all new, with the exception of *Turn*, which first appeared under the title *Benaud* in issue 14 of The Nightwatchman.

Bob is well known for his children's books about sport, including the ever-popular *Glory Gardens* series.

SECOND XI

More stories from the world of cricket

Bob Cattell

illustrations by
Bob Linney

Charlcombe Books
17 George's Road, Bath BA1 6EY
Tel 01225-335813

First published 2018

ISBN 978 1 9996558 0 8

Cover design by Bob Linney

Printed and bound in Great Britain by
CPI Antony Rowe, Bumper's Farm, Chippenham, Wilts

Contents

To Sam Sheringham

TURN

TURN
Australia

"I thought you were the man from the Urban Utilities," said Mrs Benaud.

"Why?"

"He was due this morning. Between 9 and 1 ... they said. Otherwise I wouldn't have let you in."

He looked at her blankly, standing there right in the middle of her sitting room. He had pushed past her when she opened the door. Not aggressively but definitely a push.

"What do you want?" she said.

He was youngish – probably early thirties. The flesh of his face and neck still firm but his features gave the hint of the older form he would grow into. Not an unkind face. Blond hair, slightly plump. But his eyes told another story – black, dead, but always on the move like the eyes of a cornered animal. And Mrs Benaud cursed herself for opening the door to him.

"It was the name on the bell," he said.

"What?"

"Benaud."

"Yes?"

"You related?"

She looked puzzled.

"To Richie Benaud, I mean? ... 'spose not. Stupid question," he added.

"Yes, his niece."

It was a barefaced lie. She had, of course, been asked the question hundreds of times before, and until now

9

she'd always answered with a straight bat, so to speak. Not only was she not related but, famous though he was, she knew practically nothing about her namesake except for the obituaries. She'd read a couple of them when he died.

She lied out of instinct. This young man was an intruder and he scared her. She sensed it was best to keep him talking …

"Wow, Richie Benaud your uncle!"

In a flash the moment of exhilaration passed and the hunted look returned to his face.

"I shouldn't have dragged you into this."

"Into what?"

"N…never mind." His right hand jerked suddenly to the pocket of his bomber jacket. A gun, she thought? Or a knife?

"I don't see any pictures of him …" The haunted eyes darted around the sitting room at the family photographs, which covered most of the polished surfaces.

"Er … no. I used to have a nice one of him with my mother, but someone took it."

"Nicked it?"

"No. I think my son borrowed it."

"I bet you saw him play loads of times."

She shook her head. "I'm afraid I'm not really that interested in cricket."

She could sense the danger. And she tried to scour her frightened memory for the few scraps of information she had. Cricketer and commentator. He'd been 84 when he died – for some reason she remembered that. Skin cancer. And he'd been Australia's most successful cricket captain as well as a popular TV commentator. But that was about it. She decided to wing it. Let the game of bluff begin … no matter what the stakes. And, to her surprise, that was the moment she realised she was no longer afraid.

"I saw him play here once when I was a girl. The whole family went."

"At the Gabba? Was it a test match?"

"Yes. Against England, if I remember rightly."

"When?"

"Well let's think … I was 12 or 13. So it must have been the late fifties."

"1958," he said triumphantly. "That was his first test as captain. Boy, the 4 – 0 Ashes victory. And you were there?"

"Yes. You're right. He turned out to be a natural captain. But I'm afraid I can't remember much about it … except I took a book and my dad told me off for reading while Uncle Richie was bowling."

"So England were batting. I guess that would be day one … their first innings. On the Friday. The poms were so cocky. They reckoned it was the best team ever to leave England. Peter May, Cowdrey, Graveney, Dexter, Subba Row, Godfrey Evans. And the bowlers? Trueman, Tyson, Statham, Laker and Lock. They were the invincibles. And we hammered them, all thanks to Richie."

"How come you know so much about it? For heaven sake it's ancient history … long before you were born.

"My dad told me. Dad was Richie Benaud's biggest fan. He even met him once as a boy … face to face like. He won a newspaper competition and got to join him in the commentary box. He said Richie was a real gentleman and he talked to him about cricket for ages."

"Does your father live in Brisbane?"

"No, he's dead. And that's it, see. He died the same day as your uncle. April 10th. Some coincidence, eh? I expect you were at Richie's funeral."

"Well, eh … no. I was in hospital having a hip operation." The lies were multiplying, tumbling out of control.

"A state funeral, they called it. Dad's was just the opposite. A few friends came … none of the family except me."

"I saw it on telly later … Uncle Richie's funeral, I mean."

"Everyone loved him, and it all started that day at the Gabba. England bowled out for 134. Did you see Davidson and Meckiff bowl?

"Well now, I don't know … I suppose I must have."

"They both took three wickets. Benaud kept them on while the ball was swinging. Davidson had to leave the field with heat exhaustion and Richie came on himself and took three wickets to finish the rout. Three for 46."

"My, you are well informed. And to think I was there and I can hardly remember a thing."

"Did your uncle talk to you about cricket much?"

"No." Then she remembered something … he had been a betting man. "Of course, we talked about horses a lot. I like to put a little bet on most days. He was most knowledgeable. Gave me a lot of tips. Once at the Sydney Autumn Carnival he …"

A police siren sounded in the street below and the young man rushed to the window and pulled the lace curtains back to peer out. Of course, that was it … he was on the run. What dreadful crime had he committed?

"I don't know why you're here …" she began nervously. "But I wish you would tell me. Are you in trouble?"

He appeared not to hear the question and continued to gaze down at the street. Then he turned to face her. Suddenly he seemed a lot older, more careworn.

"My dad left my mum when I was still at school," he said, fixing her with those dead eyes. "She'd already started drinking and she told him she'd met someone else. It didn't last. But then she got a divorce and married ..."

"Who?"

"Him. The monster. I can't even say his name. He took her over. She was never the same after he moved in."

"Were you living with your mother?"

"I left when I was 18. Went to live with dad."

"And what happened?"

"The monster beat her. It happened first when they were both drunk. But then it was all the time. He hit me, too. That's why I moved out. I begged mum to go to the police. She did once but, when he said it would never happen again, she withdrew charges. Of course, it was a lie, like all his other lies."

"Where do you live now ... now your father's ...no longer ..."

"I sold his house and bought an apartment – not as nice as this one, but big enough for me."

"Have you got a job?"

"Not now. I used to work as a baker ... but after dad died I couldn't get up in the morning. They were decent people but in the end they fired me."

"I was a chef," she said.

"What, here in Brisbane?"

"I worked all over. Paris, London, Cape Town, La Botte d'Oro in Sydney. Then I came full circle and fetched up back in Brisbane until I retired ... at Montrachet."

"That's pretty swanky."

The noise of the police sirens seemed to reach a crescendo. She took a step towards the window but he grabbed her by the upper arm and dragged her roughly away.

"Sit down! They might shoot," he said. And then more gently. "I don't want you getting hurt."

She sank back into her chair. A pain shot up her arm. Whatever he had done, it was serious enough to have sparked off a major police operation. She could hear loudspeakers in the street, warning people to keep clear. She imagined the street cordoned off, news cameras, her neighbours evacuated and talking to the journalists. What had this young man got himself involved in? Terrorism? Drugs? Murder? She decided it was time for some new tactics.

"Are you hungry?"

He looked surprised at the question.

"I cook a very good omelette. Uncle Richie used to tell me my omelettes were the best in the world and, as you know, he travelled everywhere. Ate at the best tables. Strictly speaking I was a pastry chef, but I promise you I can do the best omelette and salad in Brisbane. I've got a bit of ham on the bone too. It's very good."

"Ok," he said quietly. "Maybe I am a bit hungry. But ..."

"Coming up," she said with a smile.

He peered out of the window again, then followed her into the kitchen which led directly off the sitting room. She put on her apron and turned up the burner on the oven. He sat at the large oak table. Out of the corner of her eye she could see that his hand kept straying to the jacket pocket.

As she cracked and mixed the eggs, she talked. "I learnt this method in Normandy, from a friend who worked at the famous *La Mere Poulard.* But I've experimented with it over the years … it's a bit thicker than usual, like a cross between an omelette and a soufflé."

She had some left-over peas and broad beans … plenty of lamb's tongue lettuce, parsley and cress and artichoke hearts. That would be the basis for the salad. He sat silently watching her, and she knew it was time to spring the question.

"Tell me what you've done," she said, without looking at him.

He put his head in his hands. She started gently beating the eggs, her attention on the job in hand. There was a little choking noise and she wondered if he was weeping.

"I shot the bastard," he said suddenly.

"Your step-father?"

"Yeah."

"Tell me about it."

"I went to see Mum … I hadn't been round for a couple of weeks. Because I knew he was out of work and at home a lot. She was sitting in the kitchen, blood running down her face and a big bruise coming up under her eye. She looked terrified when she saw me, and then he burst into the room, like a mad bull, roaring obscenities and coming for me and I pulled out the gun and shot him. Once … then three more times. Mum was screaming. I didn't know what to do … so I ran. Got back in the van and scarpered. I hated myself for it … leaving her like that."

"Where's the gun?"

He tapped his jacket pocket.

"Let's see it."

He pulled out a small hand pistol, placed it on the kitchen table and sat staring at it.

"Do you always carry a gun?"

"No. I bought it last week. For protection. In case he … But I didn't mean to kill him, honest. Just warn him off like."

She seasoned the eggs, added a pinch of grated Parmesan.

"I've never laid a hand on anyone … not since I was a kid. Which is why this is so strange. I thought there was this wall between violence and loving peace, but when I leant on the wall I went straight though, like it was made of paper."

She was about to pour the mixture into the heavy-duty frying pan when the phone rang. It sounded twice as loud as usual. She hesitated and then went to answer it.

"Leave it."

"But …"

"Leave it. It's the police. They know I'm here."

"So talk to them. It's best you …"

"I shot a copper."

"You did what?"

"He came after me on his motorbike. I must have been speeding or something. But I got confused. I thought he was chasing me for the …. Stupid. Mum wouldn't have rung the police. And anyhow they couldn't have been onto me that quick."

The phone stopped ringing. Then her mobile started its silly ring tone. *Under the boardwalk.* He grabbed the gun.

"Turn it off."

She fumbled for the phone in her handbag and silenced it. "Did you kill him?"

"The cop? No. He came alongside, shouting at me to pull over. I shot him in the leg and he fell off his bike. I saw him in the mirror trying to stand up."

"So when the police break in here, what are you going to do? Use me as a hostage? Shoot it out and get both of us killed?"

"No." He rapped out the word like a sergeant major on parade. "You won't be hurt. I don't care what happens to me."

"Then let's have lunch and, when they phone again, will you trust me to answer it?" It rang almost immediately. He nodded slightly and looked away. She picked up the receiver. As she put it to her ear she switched on the loudspeaker.

"Mrs Maria Benaud?"

"Yes."

"Are you safe, ma'am?"

"Perfectly."

"Is there someone with you? A young man, blonde hair …"

"Yes," she interrupted. "And if you want to talk to him, I suggest you ring back in exactly one hour."

"But I'm warning you, ma'am, you're in great peril. He is armed and dangerous."

"I'll be in far greater peril if you try and arrest him now. So please do as I say. Keep well away from my apartment. I am not in any current danger. Will you ring me again in exactly one hour?"

"But, ma'am …"

"Please do as I say."

She put the phone down, picked up the egg mixture, gave it another gentle stir and poured it into the heated frying pan.

"What difference will an hour make?" he asked in a voice that seemed to come from a long way away.

"I don't know. But whatever you're going to do, you're not doing it on an empty stomach. I promised you a meal and you're going to eat it."

"The cops won't take any notice of you."

"I think they might. I can't imagine they want the death of an innocent hostage on their hands."

"You're not a hostage."

"Then what am I? Free to leave?"

He stared at her with those dead black eyes. "What would Richie do in a situation like this?"

"You tell me. What made him such a good captain? How did he win all those games?"

"That's the thing. Whenever he had his back to the wall he went on the attack. Take that game here in Brisbane against the West Indies. You must remember that one."

She gave an inconclusive nod and drew the mixture in from the sides of the pan with a wooden spatula.

"We were six for 92 on the final day chasing a target of 233. Benaud and Davidson at the crease. Attack, Richie decided … was their best chance of survival. First with quick singles, then a mix of boundaries."

As he spoke she began to hear the cadences of the radio commentator, probably learned from Richie Benaud himself. A voice abandoned to the cut and thrust of the battle on the pitch at the height of its intensity.

"They took the game away from the West Indies. Between them they put on 134. Only seven runs required but time was running out."

She wondered why time was running out, but she decided against interrupting him.

"Benaud drove into the covers, and they went for a quick single. A direct hit from Joe Solomon and Davidson was run out. Last over of the game. We need only six to win. Then disaster. Richie goes for the hook and is caught by the keeper for 52. Another run out and, with the scores level, Joe Soloman runs out Meckiff with another direct hit. A tie. The first tied test match in the history of the game."

"Wonderful … so maybe you too can get away with a tie if you play your cards right."

"What's the point?"

"For your mother maybe?" She watched his face dissolve as if it had been melted with acid and felt she'd pressed the wrong button.

"Come on, it's time to eat."

She tilted the pan and let the omelette fall to the edge. Expertly rolling a third of it over, she tipped it onto a plate. The salad, the ham and a glass of red wine were already on the table. She sawed off a couple of slices of her own sour-dough bread and beckoned him to start eating.

He ate absent-mindedly but ravenously. Mumbling his appreciation of the food between mouthfuls. She watched him and wondered. There was only one solution to the mess he had got himself into. He had to give himself up and then find a good lawyer. But would he listen? She realised finally she had to level with him.

She waited till he had almost finished eating and said, "There's something I need to tell you."

"Mmm … where did you get this bread?"

"I made it."

"It's delicious. Will you show me how?"

"I will … if we remain friends. So now you know I can cook."

"You bet."

"But there's plenty you don't know about me."

"For instance?"

She decided to risk it. "For instance, that I'm not Richie Benaud's niece. I'm not related to him in any way."

"So why …"

"I was frightened. I thought you meant me harm. I lied to you. But I'm not sorry I did because, if I hadn't lied, you wouldn't have told me those lovely stories."

He sat silently staring at her.

"Will you tell me your name?"

"Robbie Miller."

"Not a bad name for a baker."

"An ex-baker."

She looked at her watch. "Well Robbie, we've got exactly five minutes before the police ring. Would you like another glass of wine?"

He shook his head, stood up and went back to the living room window. She collected up the dishes and carried them to the sink. When she looked again he was staring defiantly at the scene below. How many cops were out there on the street now, she wondered? A high alert or whatever they called it? Armed patrols. Marksmen on the rooftops. Even if he gave himself up the moment would still be fraught with danger.

She watched as he let the lace curtain drop and slowly shuffled back to the kitchen, his head bowed.

"Time to attack. Take the initiative," she said.

"You know what?" he said. "I'll take a bet you really *are* related to Richie. You think like him."

"I take that as a compliment."

He picked up his jacket from the back of the kitchen chair and stretched out a hand to pick up the gun. She gently rested her hand on his.

"I'd feel a lot safer if you left it there," said Mrs Benaud.

He nodded and relaxed his grip. The phone rang.

"Will you come with me?" he said.

"Yes."

BOWL

BOWL
South Africa

It wasn't that Fat Norman actually thought he was Dale
Steyn – at least, I don't reckon he did. But whatever got
into him that afternoon left its mark on everyone who was
there.

Fat Norman wasn't really that fat. Not fat like Hadrien
Buitendag or Russ Meyer in year eleven. But he had the
sort of flesh that wobbled and didn't look part of him, if
you get what I mean. He certainly never looked healthy.

Naturally, the other kids picked on him. Norman was
an outsider and they let him know it. There were songs
and chants which everyone in the class could recite, such
as:

>Stuck in the door, man
>Can't get off the floor, man
>Pig sized
>Big thighs
>Whoa! Fat Norman!

Norman responded to these taunts either by sticking his
nose haughtily in the air and walking away with a smirk
on his face or charging like a mad bull and head butting
his closest adversary in the guts or lower. You never knew
which it would be and for the rest of the class that was a
large part of the fun to be found in bullying him. But not
for me.

I didn't fit in much better than Norman. I wasn't
interested in playing rugby or looking at pictures of girls on
my phone or drinking lager. And, though I loved cricket,
my passion for the game was limited to watching it on TV

– I was hopeless at playing it. Looking back on those days I must have come across as the archetypical computer nerd, a persona reinforced by my Indian ancestry, thick glasses, skinny body and unruly black hair. I countered bullying by keeping my head down and making myself scarce but I couldn't help being impressed by Norman's more high-viz approach.

I was supposed to be Norman's only friend. It wasn't really a friendship, however, more of an accident. It happened because we lived next door to each other in two identical suburban houses. And we were both brought up by our single mums. My dad died five years ago. I never met Norman's father; there was some story about him running off with a woman bus driver on the 216 route to Sunningdale when Norman was two.

Our mothers grew close out of need. Because of their jobs and other commitments, they became dependent on each other for shopping and school and work travel arrangements and they then took to drinking large quantities of wine in each other's houses in the evenings. As a result Norman and I got forced together. Of course I knew he was strange and part of me hated him, but life was rarely dull when you were in Norman's company and that was important to a 15-year-old boy, particularly when little else was happening in the neighbourhood.

Norman introduced me to Wagner. When his mum was out he would play 'The Ride of the Valkyries' or what he called the 'Demolition Scene', when Brünnhilde sets fire to Valhalla. He would turn it up to full volume and march up and down shouldering his dad's 303 rifle. His mother took the gun away from him after he blasted a massive hole in the back of her sofa, where I had been

BOWL

sitting only moments earlier before moving to look out of the window because I thought I heard my mum coming home. Norman eyed up the sofa as if it were a charging rhino and then let it have it point blank. The blast was deafening, and Norman was knocked over backwards by the recoil. It had never occurred to me before that the gun could have been loaded.

The sofa incident wasn't a one-off. Danger was always present in those days as I joined only semi-reluctantly in Norman's fantasies. One stunt involved climbing out of a window onto the roof to escape an ISIS attack led by Caliph al-Baghdadi. On another occasion we crossed the river by the school on a precarious structure of planks and branches and ropes to avoid the clutches of Spider Man. Norman hated spiders.

He didn't like birds much either. Once, during an unusually lively physics lesson, Norman stole a lump of potassium from the Physics Lab. Old Polly van Huisen was showing us what happens when you chuck potassium into water. He must have calculated the quantity wrongly because the resulting flash nearly lifted off the lab roof and the front row were simultaneously blinded and soaked with water. Rather than try a mere repeat of Polly's experiment, Norman split his piece of stolen metal into small pellets, wrapped them in bread and fed them to the pigeons. We watched two birds explode in mid-air in disgusting feather bombs.

By comparison the many hours we spent playing 'Owzthat' seemed blessedly safe and peaceful. The game had belonged to my dad, and we'd played it together a few times the Christmas before he died. Norman was less than enthusiastic about it at first but soon we were taking each other on at every opportunity. And when Hanze Knoetze, the creepy head of sport, spotted us playing it one lunchtime he almost wet himself with joy.

"Good heavens, 'Owzthat'," he exclaimed. "It's decades since I've seen that. I used to play it all the time when I was a kid."

That was a turning point. Norman re-christened the game 'Nasty Knoetze' and we played endlessly, keeping score of every match.

'Owzthat' is a simple and totally unskilled game. There's a batting side and a bowling side and two long dice with six sides. The batter rolls the die with numbers on the faces – 1, 2, 3, 4 and 6 representing runs scored as well as the fatal appeal 'Owzthat'. You go on totting up the runs on your scoresheet until you roll 'Owzthat'. Then it's the bowler's turn. He has a similar die with the options: Bowled, Caught, Run Out, LBW and also Not Out and No Ball. So the batter is usually given out, but there is a one in three chance of a reprieve.

As the games evolved, Norman and I took on the role of captains of the opposing teams and we would pick our teams alternately. He was always Dale Steyn, captain of South Africa A, and I would be Hashim Amla, captain of South Africa B – though we swapped the A and B around every week for fairness. Why Norman identified himself with the country's greatest fast bowler is anyone's guess, but Hashim Amla had long been my hero – Hashim had grace, timing, exquisite poise, everything I lacked.

As we picked the teams Norman's first choice was always another aggressive fast bowler: Morne Morkel or Vernon Philander. I usually went for an all-rounder – sometimes Chris Morris, sometimes JP Duminy. Once we had written down the full eleven players on our score sheets, battle commenced.

We played obsessively and the archive of score sheets, secretly photocopied by Norman in the school secretary's office, mounted up over the weeks and months. When we reached the 100-games mark Dale's team had won 53 games and Hashim's 46 with one (very exciting) tie. At 200 games Hashim led by one, thanks to an unprecedented run of ten wins on the trot which drove Norman mad.

Over the weeks the contests became more and more aggressive. We hurled the metal dice down venomously on the table like Chinese gamblers in a heated game of Mah Jong. The screams of 'Owzthat' grew louder. And then the sledging crept in. Dale Steyn's batsman abuse was the most extreme, but both de Villiers and de Kock behind the stumps contributed a spicy running commentary, often verging on the obscene. Hashim Amla, however, always remained polite, silent and aloof in the face of extreme provocation.

Whenever we were playing Norman refused to speak to me unless I addressed him as 'Dale' or 'Steyn Gun' or one of the many nicknames he made up for his hero. Norman also developed a passable imitation of Steyn's voice and walk. He always wore the number 8 green-and-yellow South African ODI shirt when he played 'Nasty Knoetze'. And he even attempted to grow a weird little Dale Steyn beard, but it made him look like a rodent with terminal acne. His victory celebrations, also modelled on Steyn, involved endless arm pumping with the veins sticking out on his forehead.

One day Hashim was facing up to Dale. South Africa B was on a creditable 55 for one and, after the early wicket of Stephen Cook, Amla was finding his form. He had already scored 39 when I rolled an 'Owzthat'.

"Got you, you beardy, bald bastard," shouted Dale and threw his die onto the table. The silver hexagon rolled to 'Caught' then teetered on the edge and tipped over to 'Not Out'.

"Umpire," screamed Dale. "That was bloody out!"

"Didn't carry," I said and rolled again. Another 'Owzthat'!

Norman beamed. His cylinder smashed against the wooden table top and rolled to 'No Ball'.

A cry of anguish, followed by a barrage of profanities.

I threw. "Six."

That was too much for Norman. He slammed his fist on the table, tore up his score sheet, called Hashim every racist name in the book and stormed out of the house. Moments later I heard 'The Ride of the Valkyries' blasting out across the neighbourhood.

I forgot to say that Norman was under a cloud at school for his erratic behaviour. His mum had already received two written warnings from the headteacher, Alka 'Hard' Butt. A third and, everyone said, he'd be out – sent to De Groote, the special school for uncontrollable and disruptive kids. That seemed only to encourage the other kids to bully and provoke Norman the more. It also put an extra responsibility on me.

"You're the only one he listens to," his mum said to me. "Try and keep him out of trouble."

But what could I do? No one could control Norman because no one had a clue what was going on in his head.

I wasn't with him that afternoon in the last but one week of the summer term. The exams were over and we were being subjected to the so-called 'educational pursuits' that occur when teachers are treading water in the countdown to the holidays – visits to museums, art galleries and dubious historical monuments.

On the day in question the Cape Town Cricket Club was providing fielding, batting and bowling practice sessions on the playing field by the school for the entertainment of anyone in years 9 to 12 who was interested. My eyesight and lack of co-ordination made it a non-starter for me, but I watched for a time. Some of the top batters in year 12 were facing up to deliveries of 140 kilometres an hour from a bowling machine the Cape cricketers had brought along. Side-on I couldn't even see the ball as it flew out of the robot-like contraption.

When I came back from a cigarette in the out-of-bounds wood behind the tennis court, the cricket session had come to an end and everyone had gone off for showers and drinks.

Later, before the end of school, we had a roll call on the parade ground, which lies between the gym and assembly hall. At the far end is the boiler house, with a staircase at the back leading up to a flat roof where the water tanks are located.

Hard Butt had just launched into one of her tedious 'thoughts for the day' – about self-control and responsibility, if I remember rightly – when there was cry and a boy two rows in front of me sank to his knees. I saw the next missile just before it ricocheted off Hanze Knoetze's shoulder. We were under attack. From cricket balls!

People were running everywhere; some pointing at the boiler house roof. And here was another one, a fast, low in-swinger. It was coming straight for me like a heat-seeking Exocet but at the last second I ducked, and it caught Mo

Prakhana smack on the nose. Over the sounds of the crack of leather against bone and Mo's whimpering I heard a loud cry from the direction of the boiler house.

"Phalaborwa!"

Instantly I knew it was Norman on the roof firing cricket balls out of the bowling machine, cranked up to 150 kph … Norman as Dale Steyn screaming out the name of the small town the South African star grew up in, way out in the bush. Phalaborwa.

There was chaos in the crowd as the rate of the volleys increased. Some lay flat on the parade ground floor playing dead and were sitting targets for the cricket-machine sniper. Most ran for cover towards the bushes alongside the gym. A small counter-attack group of prefects circled round towards the boiler house stairs.

The police arrived in riot gear but, before they could storm the rooftop, the hailstorm of balls ceased. Either Norman had run out of balls or the machine had jammed.

In the final tally the number of serious injuries was lower than I'd expected: two people sent for treatment with concussion and one broken arm, a suspected broken nose and some nasty lacerations suffered by a girl running through a plate-glass door in her haste to get away. But plenty of bruises were notched up – Hanze Knoetze, who was hit three times, looked as if he'd been in a street fight.

As for Norman, he was last seen with a blanket over his head being bundled into a black-windowed police van. He's now attending the De Groote as a boarder. Within two months of the incident his mother moved house. And I never set eyes on either of them again.

YIPS

YIPS
Ireland

When Corinne received her two-book contract she thought getting published was the easiest thing in the world.

It had taken her nearly four years to write the novel, but a friend found her an agent almost immediately. And then, despite the warnings that publishers were not taking on new writers these days, in the course of three miraculous weeks she had not one but two offers of publication. The first thing she did, after receiving her contract from Random House together with a healthy advance, was to give up her tedious job with the advertising agency to concentrate on book two.

That was twelve months ago. And now the first novel would be out in a couple of weeks and she was heavily involved in a round of pre-publicity events, mainly consisting of local radio interviews in far-flung parts of the country. The book was a thriller set in New York, a city Corinne knew well because her father had lived there for the past 15 years, ever since he left her mum. As a teenager, she had learned to hate and then love the city during the long stretches of school holidays that she spent with her father. A New York publisher had just picked up the American rights to the book, so she was looking forward to another visit shortly.

However, after months of research and false starts, she still had no idea where the second novel was coming from. There was plenty of time – nearly a year going by the contract – but the failure to get even a foothold on the plot was beginning to prey on her mind and keep her awake at night. She had half-decided to set the new book in Los Angeles and had written a rather violent drowning episode on Malibu Beach, which she must have read and edited a hundred times, some days liking what she had written and on others seeing it as melodramatic trash. And so, for weeks, fast becoming months, the new novel hadn't moved on by a single word.

She was still writing. Plenty of words were spilling out of her computer, because her limited literary fame had opened a few doors and she had received a number of commissions from newspapers and magazines as well as online blogs. The highlight was being asked to write ad-hoc film reviews for the Irish Times – and recently the chance to stand in for the caustic chief film editor when he was on holiday.

Lately she had been writing a series of short interview features for the Irish Times' sports pages: golf, rugby, athletics. A recent profile of Aileen Reid had earned her a pat on the back from the editor himself, and now she had her sights on cricket. Or rather one cricketer in particular.

She had come across his story during a phone conversation with her dad, who, being of Indian descent, rarely got through a day without a long discourse on the subject of his favourite game.

"So tell me, what's happened to Kyle Fagan?" he asked her.

"Kyle who?"

"I thought you were a sports writer."

"I just do features," she replied. She was in fact very well informed about nearly all sports and particularly obsessed with rugby and racing, but she had to defer to her dad's knowledge when it came to cricket. A dim recollection surfaced of a spin bowler from Dublin who was playing county cricket in England and had earned a game or two for Ireland last season.

"He's got the yips," said her dad.

"What?"

"The yips. Look it up."

She did…

> **the yips** *is the loss of fine motor skills in athletes. The condition occurs suddenly and without apparent explanation, often in mature athletes with years of experience. It is poorly understood and has no known treatment or therapy. Athletes affected by the yips sometimes recover their ability but many are forced to abandon their sport at the highest level.*

Further research revealed that Kyle Fagan was a young left-arm spinner who had starred for Trinity College and Phoenix CC before getting a contract with Northants just over a year ago. It was in his second one-day game for Ireland against Afghanistan that the trouble had started. He went for 27 in an over including five wides and a no-ball. Things got worse on his return to his county. His bowling action went into meltdown and, though still on the books, Kyle hadn't played a game since late May. Photographs revealed a tall, blonde-haired boy with startling blue eyes. Not Corinne's type at all, but interesting all the same.

His agent told her firmly that Kyle wasn't doing any interviews, not even for the Irish Times. She sweet-talked the features editor into upping the fee, but it got her nowhere. So she used the paper's network to obtain the young cricketer's mobile number and started hunting him down. Her persistence was finally rewarded. As she fully expected, Kyle was ground down and submitted, after countless phone calls and texts. Better still he was currently staying in Dublin. He agreed to a one-hour interview as long as there was no photographer present. That suited Corinne. They could always get the photo later, that's if there wasn't already a suitable one in the archives.

The interview was set up and on a wet August afternoon Corinne took the DART to Blackrock. Kyle had been given a break from training with Northants and was living in the family home, a flat right next to the sea. Corinne was impressed by the location.

"What do your parents do?" was her first question as he was hanging up her wet coat and umbrella.

"Ma's a GP. Father's a musician."

"In a band?"

"Dublin Philharmonic mostly. He plays double bass."

There was a large photo in the hall of a tall, greying man in a dinner jacket leaning up against a double bass. He looked fun. Kyle on the other hand didn't. In the flesh he was bigger than Corinne expected. So many of the sportsmen and women she had interviewed turned out to be on the diminutive side, with the exception of the rugby players, of course. Kyle was well over six foot with broad shoulders and long, gangly legs. But, as in the photographs, it was his eyes that caught her attention. They were the deep blue of a clear mountain sky at the end of the day – cobalt blue – and they darted at her and darted away in a mixture, it seemed to her, of anger and fear.

"I'll get you a drink. Tea or coffee?"

"Tea, please. No sugar."

He loped off to the kitchen and she went over to the picture window. The rain was lashing down over the bay, and she could barely make out the pier at the entrance to the port. She imagined the view on a clear, sunny day across to Howth and beyond.

Kyle put down two mugs of tea on a low table and slumped into a well-worn leather armchair.

"Well, you got your way, now let's get to work," he said abruptly. "I guess you've come to talk about the yips."

She picked up her mug and sat in the armchair opposite, which felt a little too comfortable for the purposes of a hard-nosed interview.

"I usually like to get a bit of background first," she said.

"Such as my middle-class upbringing and what I did at university?" he said.

"That sort of thing."

"And what about you? How'd you get to be a journo?"

He's not going to co-operate, this one, thought Corinne, so she gave in to his obvious diversionary tactics. She told him a bit about her work at the Irish Times and about the book.

He listened expressionlessly until she paused.

"So we're both of us in the bloody entertainment business," he said. "Me, a tweaker of cricket balls and you, a tweaker of sentences. Rum way to make a living, isn't it?"

She sidestepped the mild taunt and tried another tack.

"I guess I'm interested in your … erm … condition because I'm a bit stuck too."

She told him about the second book problem and how the journalism was, if anything, making it worse.

"Writer's block?" he said. "Is that it?"

"I think with me it's more laziness and, what they call, blank-page syndrome."

He raised his eyebrows. "Sounds a lot posher than the yips."

"It's just what it says: you stare at a blank piece of paper – or a screen in my case – and you can't come up with anything new or interesting."

"Perhaps you've only got one book in you."

"Maybe."

"Have you tried any help … to get you started again?"

"You name it. Freewriting, brainstorming, changing the time of day I write, writing in the pub and even mindfulness meditation."

He laughed. "Yeah, I've done that one."

It was the first time she had seen him smile. It made him look younger – not much more than a schoolboy – and then she realised she'd spent half the interview talking about herself and she rattled off some standard questions about his life before cricket.

He had studied History at Trinity – 'migration through the ages' was his subject – and he had travelled to some unusual places such as the Caucasus and Somalia and Mongolia. But cricket had overtaken his studies after he started playing for the Phoenix Firsts and he'd come away with a lowly 2.2.

In spite of the travelling he was a Dublin lad through and through. He'd had the Blackrock flat much to himself for some years because his dad was frequently on tour and his mother had moved to a practice in Skibbereen several years ago. Like Corinne he was an only child.

"Where do you live in England?" she asked.

"London. Camden Town. I tried Northampton but it was a bit shite."

"You've played for Northamptonshire for?"

"Just over a season. Last year was good. I was the second top wicket-taker at the end of the season."

"And this year?"

"Well, you know the story. I screwed up with Ireland and now I can't …"

For an awful moment it looked as if he was about to burst into tears, but he took a deep breath and started again.

"I used to be able to drop the ball on a beer mat. That's what my game was all about. Control. Obviously now I'm releasing it too late or too early or pulling it down too much or putting too much shoulder into it or not getting side on enough … what the hell – I'm bowling crap. And I might as well give up and try something else."

"They say bowling's about visualising," she said.

"Yeah, that's what's what the coaches and the psychos tell you. That your mind triggers the muscles when you visualise in the same way as if you were actually bowling. So you're conditioning yourself to put the ball where you want it. On a string."

"In theory?"

"Right. I've done all the visualising my brain will take and my bowling gets worse. Now I'm bowling sort of OK in the nets but, as soon as I get in the middle, it falls apart."

"So it's pressure?"

"I don't think so. Least, I've never seized up under pressure before. No-one knows what the yips is. Loads of spinners have had it: Phil Tufnell, Ravi Shastri. Phil Edmonds. Only it's unusual to get it early in your career so in my case it might be something different – like your blank-page whatsit. All I know is it's got to be something in my head."

"It's the same with me. When you're writing a story you always have to shape it in your head, first. Kind of living it."

"And now you can't?"

"I try every day – conditioning myself to get rid of the negative thoughts and believe 'I can do it'."

"But?"

"I can't find a story I believe in. And I can't be arsed with the characters I dream up."

He laughed. "Know what? I'm visualising steak and chips. I'm starving."

"There are a couple more questions I want to ask you."

"So join me. There's a half-decent restaurant round the corner; we can talk there. My treat."

It was more a gastro pub than a restaurant – slightly clinical with an excess of glass and chrome, and the sound of conversation clattered off the hard surfaces. Three of the tables were occupied and they chose one in the corner. Kyle ordered a rare steak and a bottle of red wine, after asking Corinne if she'd have a glass. She chose the Caesar salad.

He relaxed with his first mouthful of wine. She wasn't like any of the sports journalists he'd encountered in England – more serious, more professional. Pretty, too. He made a note to order her book – he wasn't much into thrillers but he was curious to know if she was any good.

"Does it frighten you?" he asked.

"What?"

"Failure."

She shook her head. "Nothing much you can do about it. When you've spent weeks on something and you know it's no good, you just have to tear it up and start again. And then somewhere you find the belief you can still do it and you begin once more with a blank page."

He remembered something one of the older pros had said to him. *You're at a crossroads, mate. If you can stay relaxed and confident you might get your action back. More likely you'll have to change your technique. And then there's the third option that you won't bowl again. What are your plans to deal with that?*

The short answer was that he didn't have a plan. A feeling of intoxication began to descend on him, as it often did over a good lunch, because he was greedy with red wine.

They discovered they had a mutual friend and talked about her and about living in Dublin. Corinne had a flat in Ranelagh, near the station. When they left the restaurant she felt that that she hadn't got much out of him that was interesting, and he half felt he'd missed the opportunity to invite her back to the flat again and seduce her.

The article wasn't her best – her instincts had been right. She emailed Kyle to let him know when it was going to appear but got no reply.

Over the months that followed she kept an occasional track on his career. He left Northants at the end of the season and went to Australia – 'to rebuild his action'. He got a one-season contract with Essex but only played a handful of games before drifting out of first-class cricket altogether, like so many young hopefuls.

The book was quite well received. A good, though rather short, review in the Irish Times and some on-line encouragement. But it didn't sell particularly strongly. She finally finished the second manuscript – a full nine months late. She set the story in Dublin – at the end of the Second World War – and one of the minor characters was a tall, blonde off-spin bowler who lived by the sea at Blackrock. She killed him off towards the end of the story. The publishers turned it down and reclaimed part of the advance and her agent failed to find anyone else who was interested though she told Corinne she'd approached 37 publishers.

Four years to the day after she had met Kyle (though, of course, at the time she wasn't aware of that), she found herself at the Phoenix Cricket Club with her father. It was the Phoenix v Merrion game and she had been invited to lunch by the international investment management company that was one of the club's main sponsors. Her dad was paying one of his rare visits, so she'd wangled him an invite, too, because she knew he'd enjoy it more than sitting with her in a restaurant.

The lunch was boring and it was chilly in the marquee. The morning's cricket had been less than exciting, too. She sat next to the vice-captain of Phoenix's second XI, an accountant and gnarled pro named Brian, who had played for the club since he was a boy. He was the world authority on the history of Phoenix CC which had begun quite interestingly, founded by James Stewart Parnell's father, and gone downhill ever since, as far as Corinne could see, apart from a few cricketing golden years in the nineteen-forties and seventies.

Her father seemed to be having a much better time of it, talking to a young fund manager who had tottered to the table on the highest of high heels and was knocking back the wine in a way that was likely to make walking even more of a challenge later.

It was when, well into the pudding course, Brian's history lesson approached the modern era that she thought of Kyle.

As Brian drew breath, she asked, "Did you ever play with Kyle Fagan?"

"Of course. He took eight for 49 in this very game seven years ago. I was playing too. Knocked 42, caught behind. Do you know him?"

"Slightly.

"Shame what happened to him. He was a fine spinner."

"When did you last see him?"

"This morning."

"He's here?"

"Yes. He's been coaching the junior teams this season, ever since he got back."

"Will he still be here this afternoon?"

"Probably. Ask for him in the club office."

After lunch the weather improved and she watched a few more overs in the bright sunshine with her dad. When he began to nod off she went for a walk with the vague intention of making enquiries about Kyle. But as she opened the door to the pavilion she spotted him, sitting talking to two young players. She hovered around until he looked up.

At first there was no sign of recognition but then he said, "Hi."

One of the youngsters got up and offered her his seat.

"Still writing?" he said.

"Still with the Irish Times."

"I read *A Night in Brooklyn*. It was good."

She almost failed the recognition check on the title of her own book. "Yeah. Long time ago."

"And the second one? Set in Los Angeles, wasn't it?"

She was impressed by his memory and told him the story of her brief career as an author and continuing slog as a feature writer at the Irish Times.

He had put on a bit of weight, which suited him, and there were traces of wrinkles in the corner of his eyes. He was wearing a salmon pink shirt with his Phoenix Club tie strung loosely round the collar.

"What about you?" she asked.

"Long or short version?"

"I'm not in a hurry."

"Well, I'll give you the short one, anyway. Cricket dumped me and I got a break. I joined a mate who was a theatre producer. Gambled all my tiny fortune on a West End play. And struck gold. So that's what I'm still doing. Back in the entertainment business."

"And you are working in Dublin now?"

"I'd been in London long enough. So I decided to set up an office here?"

"So the yips did you a favour?"

"You could say that. But between you and me I'd chuck it all away now for the chance to have been a great spin bowler."

"And you're coaching the youth sides."

"Who told you?"

"I'm a journo. Can't possibly reveal my sources."

He laughed. There was a comfortable silence whilst they both watched the match. Phoenix were batting and going along at under three an over. A straight six woke up the crowd a little, and then the lethargy took over again.

"Ever think of writing a play?" he said suddenly.

"What about?"

"Oh I don't know. Maybe a cricketer with the yips and an author suffering from writers' block?"

"And what happens to them?"

"You're the writer."

"A work of fiction?"

"Well, yes, or fictionalisation. That's the fashion, isn't it?"

"They meet in a flat in Blackrock and talk about failure. Is that what you mean?"

"Something like that … but I wouldn't mind changing the ending of their first encounter."

"How?"

"Tell you later, if you're free for dinner."

"Not tonight. My dad's staying."

"Tomorrow, then?"

"Yes."

DROP

DROP
India

Prakesh was late for work that evening. A gas explosion in the block opposite his apartment had closed the road, and the delay caused him to miss his regular train.

It turned out to be an unusually busy night for a Tuesday. The restaurant was already three-quarters full by eight o'clock and they were short-staffed because two junior waiters hadn't shown up.

Prakesh was taking an order at another table and didn't immediately see them arrive. But he stopped in his tracks when he first heard the voice. Rahil! A shudder ran through him as he was immediately transported back to St Joe's.

Rahil Shah – it was unmistakably him, though Prakesh hadn't laid eyes on him for 25 years or more – was sitting at the round table by the window with five other men. He was more thickly built, greying round the temples and his jowls wobbled a little when he spoke, but he still had those sharp eyes and exuded the supreme self-confidence of the ex-captain of cricket at St Joseph's. Prakesh guessed he'd come straight from the law courts opposite as he was still wearing the barrister's black sherwani and white bands. The other men at table seven were dressed in ordinary but expensive business suits.

Prakesh walked past the table twice to get a closer look. He knew Rahil wouldn't recognise him. Life had been less kind to Prakesh than to the privileged barrister, and there was little of the studious schoolboy still reflected in his middle-aged face. The computer business he had set up after leaving Karnatak University had gone bust just after his young wife died in childbirth. The baby had died, too. And mental health problems took their toll on Prakesh. He looked a lot older than his 51 years.

Only recently – four or five years ago – had he begun to get his life back on track. It hadn't been easy. The middle-aged are most susceptible, most in need of reassurance. With the lost dreams of youth goes the vigour for living. The position he took as a senior waiter in the City's top restaurant would have fallen well short of his mother's ambitions for him, were she not in the advanced stages of Alzheimer's and rarely recognised him these days. However, the job suited him perfectly because it kept him busy throughout the evening and night, still the most painful time of the day.

"Yaar, believe me we've got them on the back foot," he heard Rahil say in his exaggerated public school accent. The businessmen were lapping up his every word. "Tomorrow we bowl them the googly."

The cricket metaphor brought into focus Prakesh's memory of that fateful day. He had been picked for the school's first XI to play in the annual grudge match against MA International School. Well, not exactly picked. Two of the team's key players were injured and Prakesh was the second and youngest of two rookies drafted in from the second XI.

The day was hot, and the whole school had gathered around the boundary to cheer on their team. Lessons were always suspended for the MA game, and supporting the team was compulsory. St Joe's batted first and Rahil, opening the innings, scored a flashy fifty and was well on his way to his century before he was left somewhat stranded by a middle and then late order collapse. Prakesh came in at 10, immediately after Rahil's dismissal – an lbw decision the captain clearly thought so ridiculous that he shook his head in disbelief all the way back to the pavilion. Prakesh prodded away at the spinners for five or six overs before being run out by Jaga, their fast bowler and number 11, for just six runs. Everyone reckoned the total of 225 was 50 runs below par.

"Waiter, waiter. Here." It was Rahil beckoning him imperiously. He walked to the table and bowed stiffly.

"Yes, sir."

"Bring me two bottles of Chateau Palmer 2000," he demanded, jabbing his perfectly manicured finger at the wine list.

"Certainly, sir."

"And we'll have a bottle of champers while the claret breathes."

"Splendid idea," chorused the businessmen. Prakesh recognised one of them: a wealthy coffee plantation owner whose eldest son had recently been imprisoned for fraud. Not a nice man by all accounts.

He took the drinks order and persuaded his colleague that he'd take over table seven from him, swapping it for one of his regular tables. In spite of the unpleasant memories it evoked, he felt an urge to get a closer look at Rahil.

Rahil ordered prawns with wasabi cream, followed by braised lamb shanks in a pasanda source. For a man who was forever insisting on his Brahmin superiority it was no surprise to Prakesh that he went for the non-veg option.

There had been chicken pasta on the lunch menu the day of the match, Prakesh remembered. He'd watched Rahil help himself to a huge serving from the buffet and then issue orders to the team through mouthfuls of food. Prakesh just had a banana and plenty of water, no tea. He wasn't hungry and it was stuffy in the old military-style marquee that they used for cricket lunches and teas. What's more, he felt a headache coming on.

Soon they were in the field, and the sun was even hotter. As the quicks bowled, Prakesh was posted to the boundary at long leg, and then cover sweeper when they changed ends. Jaga got one of the openers with an in-swinger which took an inside edge into the stumps, and an over or two later there was a direct-hit run out. Then things went a bit quiet and the spinners took over. Prakesh bowled off-breaks for the 2nd XI but he doubted whether Rahil knew that. He certainly hadn't asked him. In fact, Rahil hadn't addressed a word to him all day except to direct him to his fielding positions with an imperious wave of his arm. The skipper was far too busy chatting to his first team friends in the slips to take any notice of a lowly 11th standard boy.

The match began to swing backwards and forwards. A stand of 60 and then a clatter of wickets, which was noisily acclaimed by the younger boys massed around the pavilion. In front of them in his grand rattan chair sat the revered figure of HL Thakeray, who had been headmaster of St Joseph's for nearly twenty years. With the eyes of the whole school on him, Prakesh fielded as enthusiastically as he could and nearly affected another run out with a smart throw to the bowler's end. But his headache was getting worse.

Drinks came on at the 25-over mark with the score 111 for five. Prakesh tried to find some shade but Rahil called him over.

"Sharpen up on your walking in," he commanded. "We need to cut out those twos."

Prakesh started to say something about his off-breaks. He'd taken four for 20 in the 2nd XI's last outing. But Rahil wasn't listening; he turned and walked away.

Table seven ordered another bottle of champagne. The court case they'd all been discussing was clearly in the bag, and they were in the mood for an early celebration. Prakesh caught a few indiscreet comments, especially from Rahil, boasting about some of the witnesses they'd 'kept sweet'.

He served the wine and then the first course. The prawns smelt good. Because of his difficult journey Prakesh hadn't had a chance to eat before his shift began and his stomach was rumbling. His diet hadn't been the best since his mother, who had always been an excellent cook, descended into the fog of dementia and he began to rely on hand-outs from the restaurant's chefs and snacking throughout the rest of the day. Several years of heavy drinking after the death of his family had also taken its toll, though he hadn't touched a drop of alcohol for five years.

He watched Rahil take his first slurp of red wine.

"Is it satisfactory, sir?"

"Satisfactory? It damned well ought to be at that price," said Rahil with a wave of his arm, indicating that Prakesh should fill the glasses of his colleagues and take away the empty champagne flutes.

The conversation at the table had turned to the question of prime minister Modi's monetary reforms, which were generally accepted to be an excellent move in spite of the short-term inconvenience for the vast majority of Indians who depended on the cash economy.

Prakesh served a family with two precocious children at another table. His head was beginning to ache. He'd suffered from headaches all his life. Sometimes they'd morph into fully blown migraines so he was always nervous when he felt the symptoms coming on.

He recalled the throbbing in his temples that afternoon as he picked himself up from a sliding attempt to stop a boundary. He'd got his fingers to the ball but merely managed to deflect it over the rope. In his opinion it went down as a goodish attempt but Rahil screamed at him and told him to field a couple of yards squarer, where he'd put him in the first place.

The game was now getting tense and the pressure was showing on both sides. MA's total edged over 200 but they had lost seven wickets and needed 23 off the last three overs for victory. The challenge for the home side was the opposition's captain, who was milking St Joe's spinners. If he was still around at the close, there was likely to be only one outcome.

Rahil brought back Jaga for his final two overs. But the extra pace just accelerated the run rate. Two fours put MA International on top, but immediately the two batters got in a terrible tangle and a sharp throw to the keeper resulted in another run out.

As the final over began, the score was 219 for eight. The younger supporters in the crowd behind Prakesh were chanting 'St Joe's Zindabad' in their high-pitched voices. Jaga bowled two fine yorkers at the number 10. The second of them squirted away off an inside edge for a single. With the MA captain on strike the fielders were posted out to defend the boundaries. Prakesh was at square-leg with the pavilion at his back. HL Thakeray's chair was only a few yards behind him. He could almost feel the old headmaster's breath on the back of his neck.

The MA captain refused a single to keep the strike. The fourth ball was short, and he swivelled and got enough bat on it to beat the diving fielder at long-leg. 224 and two balls to go. Jaga ran in hard and delivered another fast yorker, which the batter came down on at the last moment. No run.

Rahil rearranged his field for the final delivery. One run for a tie; two for the win. He signalled to Prakesh to come in from the boundary to prevent the single. Jaga stood at the end of his run. The crowd went quiet as he began his charge to the wicket. The arm came over. It was short outside off stump and the MA skipper stepped across to fetch it to leg. He got a thick top edge and the ball flew high in the air just backward of square. Prakesh saw it and then lost it in the sun. He ran back, but by the time he got his bearings the ball was coming down fast over to the right. He dived got both hands to it … and it bounced up. A last despairing lunge but he only got the tips of his fingers to it and the ball bounced away.

There was silence. The MA batters ran the second run before Prakesh could pick himself up. He turned to meet the glare of HL Thakeray.

"Bad luck, boy," said the old headmaster grimly. Everybody knew that the old man hated losing to MA. He rose regally to his feet and, with a look of grim acceptance on his face, gently applauded the two victorious batters who were walking off. Their victorious skipper shook hands with Prakesh as he passed. The St Joe's team followed, up the steps of the pavilion, in almost total silence but for a few polite hand claps. Prakesh brought up the rear, his head bowed and staring at his feet. He knew everyone was looking at him. The home dressing room was at the back of the pavilion, and by the time Prakesh reached it the door had already been slammed. He opened it slowly and walked in. And there was Rahil waiting for him, standing in the middle of the room hands on hips.

"Abe chutiye!" he said. "You fucking clown!"

Prakesh felt the tears forming in his eyes. He turned away from Rahil, grappled for his clothes and kit and ran. Out of the pavilion, across the field. The tears came only when he was beyond the ground in the shelter of the chemistry lab. He never played cricket again.

As he collected the first course plates on table seven, they ordered another bottle of Chateau Palmer. The conversation was getting louder and more raucous,

"Bloody Farook," said Rahil. "He's cheating on his wife again."

"Surprise, surprise," said one of the suits with a smutty laugh.

Prakesh and one of the junior waiters brought on the main course. Three of them were having lamb shanks. Prakesh placed the large dish on the table and then with serving spoon and fork carefully transferred the meat and sauce onto the heated plates. Rahil had his hands planted on the table and didn't move them to make room for Prakesh's serving operation. He carried on talking as if the waiters didn't exist.

Something caught Prakesh's eye as he was manoeuvring the last portion of lamb shank onto the plate. The spoon slipped and the meat dropped, A splash of gravy landed on the left cuff of Rahil's immaculately starched white shirt.

"What the hell! Abe chutiya!" exclaimed Rahil.

Prakesh looked into his eyes and then up at the street lamp, which shone brightly through the restaurant window like the orb of the sun.

The ball was coming towards him through the glare. He'd run too far back. He took a step forward … but it was dropping to his right. He launched himself. As he dived, the ball hit his hands inches from the ground. He felt the hard contact … the sting against the pad under his thumb. Then the jarring of his elbows and it was gone … bouncing away. He'd dropped it. Dropped the vital catch in front of the whole school. He hammered his right fist violently into the turf in anger and frustration.

There was a gasp and Prakesh looked down. He still held the serving fork in his right hand. But the prongs were embedded through the back of the hand on the table into the hard-wood surface, And a pool of blood was spreading rapidly over the expanse of the white table cloth.

OVAL

OVAL
England

That morning I arrived at the ground some little time after the beginning of play and took my seat. I did so without relish as I have no interest whatsoever in the game of cricket. The cult of games as proposed by Dr Arnold on the playing fields of Rugby and Eton seems to me to elevate such pursuits above man's intellectual endeavours in a manner which I find utterly ridiculous. Nevertheless, I had taken care to familiarise myself in advance with some of cricket's arcane rules – or Laws, as those who vaunt the greatness of the game insist on calling them.

The seat that the doctor had negotiated for me was, fortunately, in the shade and on the far side of the pavilion away from the busy entrance where hawkers, tipsters, illicit book-makers and other opportunists were noisily plying their trade. Before me lay a field of carefully mown grass on which the five-day contest was to be fought. I counted 13 moving figures dressed in shades of white or cream clothing with coloured caps and belts and two umpires officiating in their long white coats. The crowd around the boundary in the tiered bench-seating and standing areas was large and in holiday mood. Four bulky gas holders loomed ominously above the ground immediately opposite me.

I consulted the printed card I had been given at the entrance gate, where I had also ascertained that England were batting. I concluded that the large, bearded gentleman standing in the middle of the field whose every antic with his cricket bat was met with cheers from the adoring crowd was the celebrated Dr WG Grace.

It was a sultry August day and most of the people in the seats around me had dispensed with their top coats and sat in waistcoats and shirt sleeves. I kept my tweed jacket on. As much as I could make out from the puzzling arrangement of numbers on the scoreboard across the field, England were 52 for no wicket and Dr Grace was 37 not out. I later learned that the tall, spindly fellow who was sending down the ball at alarming speed was Fred 'The Demon' Spofforth, who is Australia's fastest bowler and regarded as Dr Grace's nemesis – a fact that may have explained the jeers coming from the more raucous elements in the crowd gathered on the mound to my left.

I cursed Watson again and myself for not putting up a stronger defence against his feeble arguments that a chance to see the immortal Dr Grace in person was not to be missed, particularly since it also offered the opportunity to witness the upstart Australians being defeated for the third time this summer. But it was the doctor's third point that finally chipped away at my resolve. No-one, he said, can count himself an Englishman or hope to understand the English psyche without witnessing a day at the Oval during a contest for the Ashes urn. That temptress, Curiosity, was ever my downfall and yet again I was seduced by her peculiarly unpredictable charms. The ticket had become available because Watson had been called away from London at the last minute and such were his disappointment at missing the occasion and his enthusiasm to avail me of 'this remarkable opportunity' that I grudgingly accepted.

Already I was regretting it. There were many pressing matters that I should have been attending to today, not least a second visit to Upper Swandham Lane to confront the Lascar landlord. And so, pondering on the strange case that had been occupying my mind these recent weeks, I allowed the warmth of the day and the effect of the opium I had enjoyed the previous evening to convey me into a shallow waking slumber.

I was brought rudely back to the present by a loud shout within inches of my left ear. "Well batted, sir," boomed my neighbour, an extraordinarily ugly man of average stature. He leapt to his feet and applauded enthusiastically, with the rest of the crowd around the ground, what I soon established was Dr Grace's half-century.

"Fine knock, sir," said my neighbour turning to me for affirmation as he sat down again – this time speaking in a quieter and surprisingly cultured tone which somehow accentuated his exceptionally unpleasant appearance. He was a man in his forties: short, thick-set and deep-chested almost to deformity. His bow legs, long arms and low brow, half overgrown by a mop of thick black hair, gave him an unfortunate likeness to an African gorilla.

I nodded and looked away and, as a result, glanced at the man on my other side, who, something to my relief, appeared to be wholly unmoved by Dr Grace's important milestone. The physiognomy of this fellow also attracted my attention. He was a large, well-made, smooth-faced man of fiftyish with an air of kindness but, nevertheless, in the corners of his mouth, there lurked a trace of slyness and a blackness about the eyes that spoke of fear. It was a very interesting countenance indeed.

"Are you a regular follower of cricket, sir?" I asked this gentleman.

"Hardly, sir. This is my first acquaintance with the Kennington Oval," said my neighbour, looking fixedly ahead and not showing great inclination to enter into conversation.

"And mine, too."

After a moment, however, the man hazarded a look in my direction. "Great heavens," he said in a discreet tone. "Am I addressing Mr Holmes? Mr Sherlock Holmes?"

"Indeed, sir."

"Bless me. I come here to observe the celebrated Dr Grace and find myself in even more distinguished company. It would be hard to say which of you has the more recognisable face in all of London."

I smiled politely. As always, I felt some irritation at being recognised in public. That may have been the reason – I surmised later – that I omitted to ask the man his name … for which I was to curse myself.

"And are you here on pleasure or business, Mr Holmes?"

"Neither," I said. I took out my pipe, tapped it against my right boot, filled and lit it. And then I attempted to explain the unfortunate circumstances that had brought me to spend the day at a cricket match. As I spoke I took in the traces of information on offer from his appearance. He was clearly a professional man – the dark grey frock-coat and stiff-crowned hat of the latest model – a lawyer or a doctor? A man of science certainly: the traces of sulphur on his left hand and a powdered salt of a type that I failed to recognise on the cuff of his shirt made that abundantly clear. In spite of his educated accent I took him for a Londoner from the slight hardening and shift of his vowels.

My neighbour showed a more than casual knowledge of some of my cases. He spoke of his fascination with the methods I had used to solve the Brixton Road murder and I was obliged to offer him some explanation of the details of the investigation.

Our conversation was cut short by the adjournment for luncheon. England at the end of the morning session had reached 93 for no wicket, of which Dr Grace's contribution was 79. He was applauded off the ground and up the steps of the somewhat decrepit wooden pavilion.

Both my neighbours departed for refreshment and, after finishing my pipe, I left my seat and walked around the circumference of the ground. It was not an enjoyable experience on account of the density of the crowd. I was jostled and elbowed and at last took refuge in a wooded area where some gentlemen were eating, seated on the grass, and others talking and smoking. I stood next to a group of middle-aged men, who were discussing the merits of the Australian team. It was here that I gleaned my information about Mr Spofforth, who, I gathered, had suffered an injury earlier in the summer and was not bowling at his 'demon' fastest.

Then I heard one of the group say, "Bless me if it isn't Professor Holly," as he bustled off to make himself known to a man walking past, whom I quickly noted was none other than my gorilla neighbour. Hearing his name my interest was instantly aroused. Professor Horace Holly had been the talk of London that month following his return from his discovery of the ruins of Kor. I was entertained to discover that this unprepossessing man was the distinguished Cambridge archaeologist and hastened to put myself within eavesdropping distance of the two men who were evidently well acquainted and soon locked in conversation.

The strangest rumours were circulating about Professor Holly's encounter with the lost city, said to be situated under a dormant volcano in the African jungle. The most beguiling of these was that the place was ruled by a most beautiful young queen who had discovered the secret of immortality. Of course I took such hokum with a pinch of salt, but I was eager to hear if the professor would speak of his adventures.

"I saw young Leo Vincey last week," said the fellow who had approached the professor. "He seems to have aged noticeably from his experience with you in Africa."

"Indeed, sir. He saw many things that will haunt him for the rest of his days."

"And will you be returning to Kor with a further expedition?"

The professor smiled, though it looked more like a grimace. "I think not in the immediate future."

"Are we to expect a paper on your findings, sir?"

"One day perhaps," said Professor Holly. "Now if you will excuse me, I must get back to my colleagues." And he hurried off, leaving his inquisitor looking mildly puzzled and offended,

I returned to my seat in time to see Dr Grace prod forward at the first ball after lunch. I was beginning to acknowledge that, however dull the game of cricket may be, the Kennington Oval does indeed, as Dr Watson had promised, afford some interesting encounters and insights into the peculiar characteristics of the English personality.

Professor Holly had not yet returned to his seat and my other neighbour appeared to be daydreaming – indeed such was his trance-like state that I would have considered him to be asleep, had his eyes not been wide open.

The crowd became more animated as Dr Grace executed a serious of shots which resulted in boundaries. This aroused my neighbour, and he began to question me further about the details of my life as, in his words, 'a consultant detective'.

I found myself speaking to him about the events that had been preying on my mind for the past week and of the mystery that had resolved itself only two days previously. Without, of course, revealing the name of my client and her husband, I briefly sketched out the extraordinary life of Mr Neville St Clair, a respectable gentleman with a home and family in Surrey, who had made his fortune as a remarkably successful and grossly disfigured beggar known to the City of London police as Hugh Boone. It was Mr St Clair's irrepressible urge to return from time to time to the excitement of the beggar's profession, and the associated pleasures of an opium den in Upper Swandham Lane by the Thames, that led his wife to believe that he had been murdered and resulted in the subsequent arrest of Hugh Boone.

"And how did you ascertain, Mr Holmes, that this man was living a double life?" asked my neighbour. I noticed that his face had taken on a strange pallor as I had been speaking and his hands were visibly shaking. He hung on to my every word.

"A letter," I said, "received by his wife after the alleged murder had taken place. I had to reconsider my conclusions and the evidence led me back to Hugh Boone. I took a bath sponge with me to the police station and, with the aid of a little water, I literally unmasked the beggar."

"Would that every double identity could be so easily revealed," said my friend, mysteriously.

Professor Holly returned and sat down with a nod of acknowledgement.

"Just in time," he said.

I wondered what precisely he was alluding to, when Dr Grace pirouetted on his heels and struck a ball towards the boundary, right in front of us. The fielder chased across to intercept it but failed and the ball hopped over the rope. Cheers broke out all round the ground, hats were thrown in the air and Dr Grace raised his bat imperiously to salute the applause.

I thought it rather excessive celebration for a simple boundary until Professor Holly informed me that we had just witnessed the Doctor's century. It appears hundreds and half-hundreds have some magical significance in the game of cricket.

However, a ball or two later something happened which surprised and delighted me. The Demon Bowler sent down a rapid ball to Dr Grace which he appeared to lean into and gently flourished his bat like a wand. In spite of the apparent lack of effort the ball came off the face of his bat with such force that the two fielders close to the boundary scarcely moved before the projectile passed them and bounced into the crowd. It was not the effect of the shot that attracted me but rather the beauty of the moment. Seen from a distance it was almost impossible to imagine how such a large bulky man could achieve an aesthetic action of such perfection and one which I never expected to associate with sport. This was a beauty which appeared to bring together the bowler, the batsmen and those in the field in an instant of collaboration. Of course, that was only an illusion because the Australians surely wanted nothing so much as to see the back of the great Englishman. But I contend, from the way the fielders stood and stared in admiration, that they too acknowledged that something elemental and beautiful had occurred. And for the first time, and for just this moment, I had to confess that I understood something of the praise that my friend Watson had heaped upon the game of cricket.

I was released from these thoughts by a slight disturbance to my right. My neighbour had put his top coat back on and appeared to be preparing to leave. As he pulled on his gloves I observed that he was shaking more than ever, and I had the strange impression than the backs of his hands were hairier than I had at first imagined.

"I have a pressing engagement, sir," he said rather abruptly, jumping to his feet, rushing out in front of me and the professor and almost knocking the man at the end of the row completely off his seat.

"The devil, sir, he's in a hurry," said Horace Holly. "Couldn't even wait till the end of the over."

His gaze followed the man as he headed for the exit gate. "You know, Mr Holmes, I've a good memory for faces and I believe I recognise that gentleman," he said.

I nodded.

"If I'm not mistaken he is Dr Jekyll, Dr Henry Jekyll."

The name brought to me the instant recollection of the murder last year of the MP, Sir Danvers Carew. The murderer, one Edward Hyde, had never been apprehended. It was revealed that he was, in unlikely circumstances, a close friend of the extremely respectable doctor Henry

Jekyll and that Dr Jekyll's very own walking stick had been identified as the murder weapon.

"Are you quite sure, sir?" I said.

"Certainly, Mr Holmes. I never forget a face. And I recall that there were pictures of both Dr Jekyll and his dastardly friend Mr Hyde in the Illustrated London News."

I left the Oval soon after tea. Dr Watson was mortified to learn later that I had not stayed to witness the dismissal of Dr Grace for 170 runs, surpassing, as my friend informed me, Arthur Shrewsbury's recently acquired highest score against Australia.

Over the coming days and weeks as the tragic story of Dr Jekyll became common knowledge, I was haunted by the memory of his face. Had I recognised him from the outset that day I wonder if I might have persuaded him to tell his story to me and hand himself in to the police. As it is, I shall never forget the terrified look in the poor man's eyes as he came to the realisation of what fate had in store for him.

Footnote

The England-Australia match at the Oval began on 12 August 1886. *The Strange Case of Dr Jekyll and Mr Hyde* by Robert Louis Stevenson was first published in 1886. Serialisation of H Rider Haggard's *She* began in Graphic magazine in October of the same year. The first Sherlock Holmes mystery was written in 1886 although *The Man with the Twisted Lip*, the short story about the beggar Hugh Boone, was not published till 1891 when it appeared in the Strand magazine.

DEEP

DEEP
New Zealand

It all began with this obituary that appeared in the Herald.

My friend Anna Jansens, who has died aged 99, was a noted cricketer, teacher, campaigner, author and song-writer. She was born in Munich soon after the end of the World War to a German father, Peter Jansens, a chef, and New Zealander mother, Hilda (nee Bowring), who worked briefly for the Allied military in the city. After the war, Anna's parents separated and she and her mother left, first for Britain and then New Zealand.

They settled in Ponsonby, Auckland, where Hilda married a jazz bandleader, Barnaby Casement. Anna's half-brother, Anthony, known as Anton, was born in 1924. Anna went to Auckland Girls Grammar School, where she discovered her passion for cricket as a left-arm spin bowler and natural hitting middle-order bat. It was while at school, too, that she tracked down her Maori heritage, through the line of her maternal grandmother, Mairana Bawtree, which led her to a lifelong interest in Maori history and traditional song writing.

She played cricket for Auckland from 1939 to 1949 and developed the left-arm bowler's wrong 'un, still locally known as the 'jansey'. Her best cricketing years were lost to the Second World War – when she served as a telephonist and code-breaker, making use of her fluent German, learned from her mother, and

*then as a truck driver at various stations around the
country. She matured as a star player for Auckland
after the War and would surely have been selected for
her country. However, international women's cricket
took several years to resume, and she was unlucky to
miss out on a cap for the White Ferns when England
Women toured New Zealand for a single test in
1948, coming on only as substitute fielder to take
a spectacular boundary catch, which dismissed the
English captain, Mary Hide.*

*During her cricketing years she taught History and
German at a number of schools in Auckland. She
suffered a breakdown in 1952 and this led to her
lasting battle with depression. She began campaigning
for Maori rights in the sixties and wrote several books
and a collection of poetry on the subject of the colonial
suppression of native New Zealanders. In this period
of her life she was best known for her song writing,
under the name Ataahua Huna, for the Maori folk-
rock band Kota-hit-anga.*

*Anna was married three times; twice to Abe
Linney, the lead singer of 'Kota' and, in between, to
the Lebanese film star Omar Gainsberg, the father
of both her children. Following the arrest of her
half-brother Anton, erroneously as it turned out, for
running a gay brothel she went on hunger strike and
chained herself to the railings outside the Auckland
High Court.*

*In 1985 she set up the campaigning charity,
Kainga (Home), which raised funds for Maori
women suffering from high levels of alcoholism in
rural communities. But, as a self-styled 'quadroon*

and sherry addict', she was often dismissed as a colonial outsider and attention-seeker by many of the Maori community. Undeterred by this rejection and the death of her beloved Abe in an avalanche, Anna continued to tour the New Zealand countryside handing out payments to women's groups in Maori townships.

In her own words, as a 'bionic woman', with two artificial knees, two plastic hips, a pacemaker and an artificial heart valve, at the age of 81 she walked the 1,000-plus kilometre length of North Island, from Cape Reinga to Wellington, to raise money for her charity and was joined by the cricketer, Ian Botham, on one leg of the walk.

In later life she became a virtual recluse. She continued writing, with an output of increasingly bawdy songs in Maori, English and German – one of which appeared on the second album of the punk band, Sludge.

Anna is survived by three grandchildren, Sarah, Noel and Ha Amu, and 16 great grandchildren. Her son John and daughter Barbara predeceased her.

J.L. Keely

I probably would not have seen the obituary but someone – I can't remember who – sent me a copy because for years I had been, on and off, researching a history of women's cricket in New Zealand. The fact that my own grandmother was Maori also raised the level of personal interest.

It surprised me, of course, that I had never before come across the name Anna Jansens in cricketing circles, though I did have some vague recall of this remarkable woman's other achievements. My puzzlement increased when I looked up the scorecard of the 1948 Test match between England Women and New Zealand Women – the only one played in England's tour of the Antipodes that year – and discovered that Mary Hide was caught by Kathleen Batty in the first innings and bowled in the second. There was no mention of a substitute fielder taking a catch.

I had some years previously written an article for Wisden about Mary Hide, partly because, like my mother, she had been born in Shanghai, albeit ten years earlier. Mary Hide became one of the great pioneers of women's cricket, playing in the first-ever women's Test in Brisbane in 1934 and captaining England for 17 years. She also played lacrosse for her country. In 1935 in New Zealand, she scored a century in the Christchurch Test, putting on 235 with Betty Snowball. England declared at 503 for five and New Zealand were bowled out for 44, and lost by an innings and 337.

But I digress. My next discovery was that all the scorebooks for the Auckland Women games in the late thirties and post-war years had been lost in a pavilion fire. So I was unable to check on the performances of Anna Jansens during her years at the club. There was, however, no mention of her in any of the Hallyburton Johnstone Shield games played between 1939, when Wellington took the title from Auckland for the first time, and 1949. Even in 1946/47, the first year that the four teams of Auckland, Canterbury, Otago and Wellington all gathered for the tournament, the name Jansens did not appear on a single scoresheet.

This was very puzzling and I decided to get in touch with the author of the obituary. But, when I approached the Herald for details, they had precious little information about J L Keely. Jon Keely, it appeared, had written two earlier obituaries for the paper and an article on New Zealand fauna driven to extinction by the arrival of the Maoris from Polynesia. They had no forwarding address for him but believed he lived near Dunedin. Because of their privacy policy, the Herald would not give me his phone number or email contact and I could find no leads for tracing him online.

After drawing a blank on Anna's cricket career, I began to investigate her more recent history. By this time I was inclined to think that the entire piece was a hoax. But I discovered that the Kainga charity had indeed existed and had been founded by Mrs Anna Jansens, although the organisation had been wound up in the early years of the 21st century, with some strong suggestions of financial impropriety, which had led to an unresolved court case. She had also written several songs for Abe Linney's band including this lyric, which may have lost something in its translation into English:

> Come all you young women
> In fair New Zealand
> And beat on your breast
> With the palm of your hand.
> Stand proudly in line
> And stand up for what's true
> And let it be known
> That your tribe follows you.

Anna Jansens' tempestuous on-off relationship with Abe was well documented in the tabloids of the day. The

Sunday Star had also devoted many pages to the scandal of Rentboygate, as it became known, and the newspaper played a leading role in the tragic pillorying of Anton Casement, which led ultimately to his suicide. Anna's drinking was also frequently referred to, and nearly every newspaper photograph showed her with a large schooner of sherry in her hand. In the sixties and seventies she was a tall, imposing woman with a broad but vaguely aloof smile – definitely more Teutonic than Maori. She had a liking for broad-brimmed hats, as well as safari outfits and tennis dresses, which accentuated her athletic figure.

The picture emerging was a puzzling one, and I found myself devoting a lot of my working week to the mystery. I have a South African colleague who claimed to be a great mate of Ian Botham, and I persuaded him to put me in touch with the great all-rounder. Maybe Sir Ian could recall his encounter with Anna. A few days later Both and I were talking on Skype and this is a transcript of the relevant parts of the conversation:

Me: Do you recall the charity walk in 1995?
Botham: Yes, of course. Anna was a remarkably fit woman for her age. I was used to walking 30 to 35 miles a day for charity in those days and I think we did nearly 50 kilometres that day. It was hot, too. Astonishing for a woman in her eighties.
Me: And did she talk about her cricket experiences?
Botham: Yes, quite a lot. She wasn't very pleased with the selectors for leaving her out in 1948. She told me the spinner they selected was a none-too-distant relative of the chairman of the

	selectors. But it didn't take much to persuade her to relive that boundary catch she took when she came on as sub.
Me:	Was she knowledgeable about cricket?
Botham:	Very. She knew all the international women players who were around after the War. She could recite you the batting and bowling averages of the great Phyl Blackler on the White Fern's 1954 tour of England right through to every game of the 2000 World Cup in New Zealand, which I don't need to tell you the home side won.
Me:	And what did you do in the evening after the walk?
Botham:	She drank me under the table. I've never seen a woman, or man for that matter, who could sink so much sherry in a single sitting. And next morning she was on the road before I came down for breakfast with my hangover.
Me:	Was she an alcoholic?
Botham:	No more than any of my friends.

So that got me nowhere. And I was beginning to despair of ever knowing the real story of Anna Jansens, when I made two discoveries over the same weekend.

I was staying with some wealthy friends in their large house not far from Rotorua. At lunch on Sunday I was placed next to a striking-looking woman, probably in her late seventies, whom I at first thought to be more than a touch batty. She was wearing a bright red scarf knotted round her head like a turban and alarmingly large red tinted glasses. She smelled of exotic scent and called everyone 'darling'. I don't recall how I discovered that she had known Anna Jansens, but then she told me that she had been a singer with Kota-hit-anga for a couple of years in the seventies.

"I joined Kota three months before Abe died, darling. Plenty of time for him to have a fling with me, though."

"I gather he died in an avalanche," I said.

"Spectacularly, darling. They went skiing rather frequently. Anna hated it, but Abe was never to be denied when he was looking for adventure. I wasn't there but I'm told he set off one morning, way off piste and out of his head on coke ... Anna would always say that he was a crack-head and she was a sherry-head. Some other skiers saw him just before the avalanche. They say he was shouting obscenities at the top of his voice at the gods of the mountain when there was a rumble from above and the snows buried him."

"And how was Anna after that?"

"Broken hearted, darling. She was devoted to him. You know what they say: couldn't live with him, couldn't live without him. I think she went a little off her head when he died. We didn't see much of her after that. Though we did record one of her songs. A sad ballad, I recall ... I can't remember how it went, but it'll come to me." And she began humming a tune and then shaking her head and humming another.

Later that day Lynn, my lunchtime companion, introduced me to a man who looked like a retired bank manager, dressed in the compulsory red chinos and crumpled white linen jacket of the rural middle class male of a certain age. Michael Battye was his name. He had been an A&R manager in the seventies and eighties and had known Anna at the time. But it also emerged that he was well acquainted with the mysterious JL Keely.

"Strangely enough I saw Doctor Jon only last week," he told me. He's in Auckland, staying with his daughter." And he went on to tell me about the writer of the obituary.

JL Keely, 'Doctor Jon', had been a director of Anna's charity. He was a professional fund-raiser and much of the criticism for the financial mis-management which led to the collapse of *Kainga* was laid at his feet. Soon after the demise of the charity he converted to Roman Catholicism and became a priest. Anna and he remained friends, and there was talk of a closer relationship. With his growing passion for the protection of wildlife species, Keely, who had established strong media contacts during his days with *Kainga*, began to write campaigning articles for popular magazines. But obsession with the rights of animals and his growing mysanthropy didn't endear him to editors and his career as a journalist was short lived. As far as Michael knew, Doctor Jon had been one of the few people to remain in touch with Anna till late in her life. He now lived in a cottage by the sea just outside Dunedin.

It turned out Keely was still staying with his daughter when I returned to Auckland and Michael managed to find her phone number for me. 'Grumpy' and 'unpredictable' were the words that Michael had used to describe Doctor Jon, so I wasn't expecting an easy ride. When I rang, he showed no interest in talking to me. But when I told him that I was writing a piece on Anna Jansens' career as a cricketer, his tone changed. We arranged to meet at his daughter's house, and when I arrived he was alone.

Doctor Jon bore a striking resemblance to Samuel Beckett except that his face was even more wrinkled and his teeth were in a worse state of repair than the great writer's. He came straight to the point.

"You read my obituary of Anna?"

"Yes."

"And?"

"I noticed a number of discrepancies."

"Relating to her cricketing years?"

"Yes."

Keely beckoned me to an armchair in the small sitting room and sat down opposite me. He had a mug of tea or coffee on the table but he didn't offer me anything.

"I knew her well," he said, in a surprisingly tender voice. "As you know she died aged 99, but you may not have realised that she was a day short of her hundredth birthday. Deprived of her century at the final gasp."

I nodded and was about to ask him a question about Anna's playing years for Auckland when he said quietly, "It was all lies, of course. I got caught up in it. In the end I think I believed it too."

"She didn't play at all?"

"I believe she had a few games for Auckland before the war. But she wasn't good enough to keep her place in the team. She loved cricket and, when the charity went under, I think those stories saved her life. She spent a lot of time on her own and people worried about her. But if you saw her in company, even in those days, she was the life and soul of the party. That's when the cricketing tales began."

"She made it all up?"

"Not all at once. She told a story here and there and steadily, over the years, they mounted up. She had a remarkable memory and, once she had invented her role in a game, she never forgot it and it became part of the overall narrative. She loved cricket and wanted to be part of the cricket family, you see."

"But why didn't anyone notice?"

"I think she was lucky at first. The people who knew the truth died; the Auckland Women's records were destroyed, as I'm sure you have discovered."

"Accidentally?"

Doctor Jon laughed for the first time. "Yes, as far as I know. But I wouldn't have put it past Anna to have torched the pavilion."

"And no-one saw through her stories?"

"Not a soul. I suppose that her narrative grew so gradually that no-one noticed. She was nearly caught out by the onset of the computer age with its thirst for data. But by that time she was an expert at protecting her reputation, and she dedicated her life to feeding false statistics and anedotes, first to Wisden and then Cricinfo. It became her passion."

"Why did you let it appear in the obituary?"

"Because she asked me to. I could never deny her anything, you see. She was, after all, a very remarkable woman who achieved a great deal in her life."

"But it wasn't enough. She had to create that fabric of …"

"Of lies. Yes. But to the best of my knowledge it hurt no-one. What's the harm in the history of New Zealand women's cricket being marginally revised? It happens all the time with history, doesn't it? And it helped her retain her sanity as she grew old."

I had run out of questions and Doctor Jon was sitting there staring into the middle distance. I was not particularly shocked by his revelations, but I had a sense of something being out of kilter in a way that could not be fixed. Not by me, anyway.

Suddenly he looked at me and said, "If you destroy her reputation, I'll have to kill you." A faint smile was playing round his lips but I wasn't at all convinced he was joking.

TIME

TIME
West Indies

She was late. No, that's not right, the damn bus was late and she was thinking, it's going to cost me another job. Care of old white people – because they mostly were white and rich and the agency took their money and paid her nearly enough to survive – that was the job and she'd been putting up with the shit that came with it now for three years.

When she arrived – even later than she had feared – she knocked on the door and there was no answer. She looked about. It was a smart new house in Stanmore Crescent with a car port and no car in it and a little front garden with plants giving the impression they were not too much cared for. She noticed it went by the name of 'Casa Blanca', though she'd just been told to go to number 22.

She knocked again. Fuck, she thought, I come all this way to miss her. Once more, louder this time and she waited. Nothing. Then there was a noise. Someone scrabbling about, rattling a key. The door opened.

She guessed he was what the agency called the 'end client'. He looked like Ronnie Wood on a bad day, only with even deeper lines around the eyes and a hunched back and wispy white beard. Ronnie Wood meets Dumbledore.

"I come see Mrs Wilmshurst."

"That's my daughter. She's gone out. What you want?"

"I come back another time."

"No, hold yer horses."

He eyed her up and down. She mumbled something about the bus. Said she'd make another appointment.

"Ah, I get it. You're one of those the bloody carer women she sends for?" he said. He asked her in. Almost pushed her through the door.

"Don't know where the fuck she's gone but she'll be back. You might as well have a cuppa. Then you can see what a miserable old git I am, and you can tell her to piss off with her job, eh?"

He was English, with an old style cockney accent. Walked slow with a limp as if his hips were going. Wheezed a bit, but otherwise she'd seen a lot worse at his age. She guessed 84 or 85.

"This is it then. Fuckin' retirement home. Stanmore Crescent. Bit of a laugh, eh? Born in Stanmore, Middlesex and I go all the way to fuckin' Barbados and end up in bleedin' Stanmore again. So where you from?"

"I live in Bridgetown."

"Been doing this all your life? Looking after smelly old gits and watching them snuff it?"

"No. Only been a carer three year."

"And before that?"

"All sort of ting. Sometimes I sing ... in clubs and bars."

"Now that sounds a bit more fuckin' interestin'."

Once she had settled down on a big white leather sofa he went off to make a cup of tea. The room was modern, polished floors, lots of glass and white walls but cluttered with photographs, mostly black and white, of people who she guessed were his family and friends. And then she saw it. It was the six sixes photograph. A signed one, too. She winced and closed her eyes. Garfield!

He came back into the room carrying a tray: teapot, milk jug, one mug and a full bottle of Mount Gay. As he put the tray down he gave her a long look as if he was seeing her there for the first time. Then his face brightened.

"I saw yer. You was looking at my photo of Sir Garry, wasn't yer? Prize possession. He give it to me hisself."

He poured tea in the mug, scratched his head and, without a word, went back to the kitchen for another one.

"Sugar?"

She shook her head.

"Well you'll have a drop of rum anyway. Always makes it taste better."

And, before she could say no, he'd poured a slug of Mount Gay into her tea and passed her the mug. She hadn't touched a drop of alcohol in three years and she resolved not to drink it. He poured an even bigger helping of rum into his own mug and sat down opposite her.

"Where was I? Oh yeah, Sir Garry ... good old Bajan geezer, eh? Everybody here tells me he's a diamond bloke. I see him loads of times in Blighty. The best was that 150 at Lord's in '73 – it was on me fortieth birthday. He blew England away that day – Willis, Greig, Underwood – and him with a bleeding hangover, or so they say. He had time, that Garfield Sobers. Time like no other batsmen I ever see. That's what sets the greats apart, see. Time ... Eh, you all right?"

She was staring at the photograph and her hand holding the mug was shaking. Forgetting her resolution she took a slurp of the tea, then another and put the mug down on the table.

"I'm sorry. But, you see, my son called Garfield."

"Oh is that right. And how old is he?"

"He dead."

"Ah. How long?"

"Five year. Six next February."

She hadn't talked about it to anyone for as long as she could recollect. Made sure to shut it away in the depths of her memory. None of her acquaintances – for there were no friends in her life anymore – knew anything about Garfield. But now it came spilling out. Perhaps because he was a complete stranger. Perhaps because of the stress of the journey and then the rum in her tea.

Garfield had been born well before she and Wesley married and just a year after they met. She was singing a lot at the Boatyard at the time. Wesley was very good looking and a little flash. She'd seen him often round the clubs and bars, but that night at the Boatyard was when it all began. After that she couldn't resist him; he was charming, funny, a bit of a risk taker, some would say chancer. It was only later that she learned he was an enforcer for the Babylon gang and supplied the beach and bar trade with crack and other highs. He had connections with the dealers in Jamaica and Bahamas and he was often away 'on business' for weeks.

After they got married and Nina was born he told her he'd split with the trade, but the money kept coming in and he wasn't doing no office job. Then he started using – all those years of dealing and he'd never touched the stuff before – and he became more and more argumentative and aggressive and possessive, especially about Garfield. He loved Garfield and he spoiled the boy terribly, whenever he had money to spare.

Their son was four years old when it happened. It was just three days after his birthday, and Wesley was driving him to his little nursery school early in the morning. At the traffic lights near Six Cross Roads a Pajero pulled up alongside them and blasted their car with semi-automatic fire. Wesley died instantly from head wounds. Garfield lasted three days in intensive care till the hospital gave up the struggle.

After that the dark descended. She started to drink heavily. She lost her job as a singer, relied on men to keep her. Nina was taken away and put with foster parents. When she hit rock bottom she had no friends, no money and nowhere to live. It was some time before she got help with her drinking but eventually she got a job with the care agency and for three years she'd managed to hang onto it, though at times it had been touch and go.

"Fuck me, that's some story," he said. He poured another ample portion of Mount Gay into his mug and waved the bottle at her. She shook her head. Then he picked up the Garry Sobers photo and examined it closely.

"So why you call the boy Garfield? You a bit young to see the great man play, ain't yer?"

"Me father love Sir Garry. When me little he forever telling me 'bout Sobers taking on Australia and England single-handed. And he tell me 'bout the time he see him score 178 not out 'gainst India at the Kensington Oval."

"1971. He hit Bedi and Vencat all over the park. And he took four wickets in the match, too."

"Wah, you know a lot about he."

"That's right. Sir Gal, he'd be my specialist subject on Mastermind. Daughter says that he's the reason why I come to Barbados to retire. Just my luck though that, soon as I get here, you lot go and forget 'ow to play cricket."

He jumped up, stood the photo back on the table in front of her.

"I got something else to show you."

He disappeared through a door into what she imagined was his bedroom. She hadn't thought about her father for a long time. Daddy hadn't approved of her singing career and he'd hated Wesley. But he'd come round a bit when his grandson was born, specially when they called him Garfield. He had just two years of bouncing Garfield on his knee and telling him stories – plenty of them about cricket and Sir Garry – and then he got cancer and was gone in a matter of weeks. Her mother followed within the year.

When the man came back into the room he was empty-handed. He stared about as if he didn't quite know where he was and he started as he set eyes on her. Then he saw that she was looking at the photograph.

"Ha, you seen my photo of Sir Garry, yeah? Prize possession. He give it to me hisself."

She stared at him but remained silent.

"It were a Gilette Cup game at Nottingham. Middlesex scored 231, Sobers took three for not much and then Notts knocked them off with time to spare. It was old Peter Parfitt, I knew him well back then, what introduced me to Sir Garry, 'cept of course he was just plain Garry in them days. I was a bit tongue-tied, what with him being my fuckin' hero like, but he gives me the photo and signs it on the spot. He says to me, this was just my party piece – meaning the six sixes at Glamorgan – but it's probably what I'll be remembered for when I die."

"I meet him too when I was young. He come to school to open the school sports day. And I talk to him one time with my daddy. I remember 'cos he have bad knees and you can see he in pain."

"I ain't seen him since I arrived but he's still living here, ain't he?"

"He have a house in St Michael, I think. Though he spend a lot of time in Australia."

"Garfield St Aubrun Sobers, he was the greatest. He had time, Sir Garry. Time like no other batsmen I ever see. That's what sets the greats apart, see. Time."

The repetition didn't faze her. It came with the job. She'd once worked for an old lady who had nurtured a beautiful garden and who had said to her a dozen times every day, "I'd love to have a big Diospyros Crassenevis in my little garden," and then burst out laughing. She'd looked up the Latin name and discovered the popular name for the plant was 'Stiff Cock'.

"Fancy a proper drink," he said. "Got some lime juice and grenadine. Could make us a rum punch."

"No thanks"

"Suit ya bloody self."

He poured another generous measure of rum into his mug and swigged deeply.

"How long you think Mrs Wi ... your daughter will be?"

"Fucked if I know. Relax. You ain't got anywhere to go, 'ave you?"

"Not specially. But I need to use the toilet."

"Nature calls, eh? Help yerself. It's the door under the stairs."

She sat on the lavatory, thinking it's time she was out of here. Can't spend the whole day with some old boy telling stories, or rather the same story, about Garfield Sobers. She washed her hands and looked in the mirror. Bags under her eyes. She retouched her lipstick and returned to the room.

"Who the fuck are *you*?" he said, voice full of alarm.

"B ... but, Mr Wilmshurst."

"I'm not fucking Mr Wilmshurst. Get the fuck out of here."

She realised she hadn't asked him his name. Wilmshurst was probably his daughter's married name.

"I come about the job."

"What job? There's no bleedin' job here. You just walk into my fuckin' house demanding work. Get out. Get out, you fucker."

He was becoming anxious as well as aggressive. It was time to leave. Fortunately, the key was still in the front door. She turned it. He was coming towards her but slowly on account of his hips. She opened the door as calmly as she could and left, shutting it quietly behind her. As she stepped into the drive a blue Fiat car pulled in and a woman stuck her head out of the side window. She had dyed, dark brown hair and a stress-lined but kindly face.

"Can I help?"

"Are you Mrs Wilmshurst?"

"Yes."

"I come about the job."

She ventured a brief outline of the past hour that she had spent with Mrs Wilmshurst's father and then explained why she had left.

"Oh dear, poor you," said the daughter. "Has he been drinking?"

"Yes, he have a spot of rum."

"It's always worse when he drinks. I try to hide the stuff. But he's a crafty old fox and he always finds it. Did he use lots of obscenities?"

"Nothing I don't hear before"

"I'm at my wits end. I can't be with him every minute of the day."

"He never remember that he forgets?"

"No."

"And it getting worse?"

"I guess so. I can't blame the carers for leaving. It gets to you, having to introduce yourself to him three or four times a day. It's like the sheet gets wiped clean every time."

"'Cept he remember all the old stuff. Like the cricket stories."

"Oh yes. No trouble with that. Well, look, I'm sorry to have wasted your time. I'd better get on and ring the agency for someone else."

"No, don't."

"What?"

"Call the agency."

"Why?"

"I take the job."

"Are you sure?"

"Yes. Quite sure."

At that moment the front door opened, and he stood there.

"Oh there you are, Daphne," he said. Then glancing at her he smiled. "Oh that's nice," he said to his daughter. "You've brought a friend back for tea."

TEST

TEST
Pakistan

He came from the high valleys of cherry trees, apricot and walnut, where Indra and Siva and Buddha and Mazda, Jupiter, Jahwe, Christ and Mohammed had fought their ancient battles for the souls of the people. The mountain passes were now a place of comparatively peaceful co-existence between the Mohammedans who venerated their living imam and whose women worked in the fields in their bright red pillbox hats and the Mohammedans who put their trust in 12 dead imams and whose women were rarely seen in the fields. Nevertheless, as people of the mountains, from time to time they all travelled to worship at the shrines just as their forefathers had done, long before the birth of Mohammed – the shrines of the Sufis, which were hated by the strict believers and the ultra-strict believers who lived further down the valley.

The name of the river that raged through his village had changed several times from its source in the high Hindu Kush and would change again before it merged its waters with the mighty Indus. Here it was called the Hunza river. Its cement-grey skin that moulded into ever changing plastic forms was witness to its dark glacial origins.

His name was Fazil. And Fazil's father, Janshir Khan, though not a rich man, was descended from the princely family and brother to the present Mir, and thus accustomed to being treated with great reverence. His influence, however, did not extend to the capital city, where he had been forced to earn his living, first as a private secretary in the Ministry of Tourism and then as director of the state tourism enterprise. Throughout his advancement he had been dependent on the patronage and goodwill of others and, naturally, such patronage did not come without a price. Janshir had thus become steadily enmeshed in the web of favours and backhanders that encompassed all who would rise in the world.

As he grew up, Fazil became increasingly aware of his father's network of shady friends and accomplices. He benefitted, through the fruits of the system, from a privileged upbringing and schooling. However, he steadily grew to dislike and then hate his father's influential friends, and this disaffection spread to his attitude towards his father. A couple of external factors were instrumental in this process. The first was his love of cricket and the second his friendship with Abdul Shakoor Mehsud.

Cricket gave him a clear, some would say naïve, perspective on life, At the age of 18 Fazil was developing into a seriously fast left-arm bowler already equipped with the skills of savage reverse swing. He was also an attacking and unorthodox middle-order batter and so possessed all the qualities desired of a modern-day T20 cricketer. Even though his career had hardly begun, people were beginning to notice him. Only last week he had received the offer from an agent of a year's contract to play for Ramsbottom in the Lancashire League in England. It was good money, and he was tempted by the opportunity to gain some experience of English conditions. But his heart lay in playing for Pakistan – Test cricket, ODIs and T20s – he wanted it all.

But cricket meant something more to Fazil. As a bookish boy he had read widely about the origins of the game from its colonial past to the present day. He was well acquainted with all the greats, from WG Grace and Donald Bradman to Imran Khan and Sachin Tendulkar. Above all, he had absorbed cricket's message of 'fair play'. Often, he would argue with his team-mates about whether a batsman should walk or a fielder own up to a grounded catch. He believed fervently that cricket depended on honesty and that it was fair play that sowed the seeds of decency.

His best friend Abdul Shakoor wasn't quite so straightforward in his approach to the game. Abdul was a crafty leg-spinner. A Pakhtun by birth and a joker by nature, he was an unlikely friend for Fazil. Abdul was short – six inches and more shorter than Fazil – and slightly built, but he made up for his lack of stature with the amount of energy he projected and the volume of noise he made. As a leg-spinner he was as full of tricks as he was in life. He bowled a googly, a flipper and a top-spinner, with no apparent change of action and with unerring accuracy, which was extremely rare for a young man learning his craft.

They both played for the City and they had also appeared, irregularly, together for the national under-16 and under-17 teams. Abdul came from a village in one of the so-called Federally Administered Tribal Areas, north-west of Peshawar. He now lived permanently in the city, and on his narrow shoulders rested the hopes of affluence of his impoverished farming family.

Like all his family, Abdul was a devout Muslim with a tendency towards the strict – though not the ultra-strict. And his beliefs came with a strong sense of humour … as he once said to Fazil, "I'm not going to try to stop you lot singing and dancing and bowing down to shrines, but it's not the way I chat to Allah."

Abdul would talk endlessly to Fazil about the dangerous topics of politics and religion and the army and how all three were locked together in a infinitely tangled embrace that was strangling the life from their country. He hated the police, the army, the ISI and the main political parties. And it wasn't long before Fazil realised that his friend, though not remotely a terrorist, was most certainly a revolutionary and could be in some danger in their fragmented country.

Abdul said to Fazil, "Trust nobody. Birds, wild animals, even cats do not trust man, and with good reason. The snow leopard, the Marco Polo sheep, the golden eagle and the chukar, they all shy away from man. And you will too when man's wickedness is revealed to you."

Abdul told Fazil about the tribal areas where his family lived. He told him that the ISI intelligence agencies were systematically killing their tribal leaders. "They use their allies in the Taliban to destroy our society," said Abdul. "They blow up our mosques, they murder our elders and it's all to create chaos on the Afghanistan border and it's funded by the Americans. We Pakhtuns are not terrorists. We are not the way we are portrayed; but hidden forces are creating insecurity in our people's lives."

Fazil listened, and he thought of his father's friends.

One of these friends was Salim Malik. He was one of the most influential and dangerous people in the city. Like many such people in Pakistan it was not clear whether he answered to the police or the army or high-up government ministers. But he knew everyone and most people believed that his strongest links were with the intelligence service, the ISI.

So when Fazil's father told him that Salim Malik wanted a chat with him, the question that hung in the air was, what does he want?

"Salim was asking after you and I told him you were looking for a career in cricket," said Janshir.

"So, why's he so interested in cricket all of a sudden?" said Fazil.

"He can help you. He's got contacts everywhere and that includes the PCB."

Fazil didn't doubt that Salim Malik could pull strings with the Pakistan Cricket Board, but that was the last thing he wanted. That ghoul only helps himself, he thought.

"And if I don't want to see him?" he asked his father. "Do I have any choice?"

His father shook his head. "Nothing to worry about. He'll send a car to pick you up tomorrow," he said.

The police Land Rover came for Fazil at the usual intimidatory calling hour, well before dawn. He was ready and dressed. It was still dark as the Defender drove without stopping through all the checkpoints into the compound and through the main entrance of an old imperial building into a courtyard. The heavy gate slammed behind them.

A few young men squatted on the concrete floor by a wall, their wrists and ankles secured. Loud music was playing from rooms behind the wall, but over the throb of sound Fazil was convinced he heard screams. He was led straight from the vehicle through a heavy steel door and along a grey painted corridor into a well-lit room lined with expensive carpets and Mughal paintings. By the single, large window, in a rattan armchair sat Salim Malik, sleek and smiling and wearing a duck blue shalwar kameez and embroidered waistcoat. So, this isn't to be a formal interview, thought Fazil, he's not got up in his army uniform.

"As salaam aleikum, meri dost," said Salim Malik, peering over his spectacles. His tone was both avuncular and threatening.

He offered tea or coffee and, without waiting for an answer, waved a hand at one of the police officers who had brought Fazil into the room; he scurried off to carry out his commission.

"How is your dear father?" asked Salim, gesturing Fazil into the identical rattan armchair facing him. "Last time I saw Janshir Khan he was up to his old tricks. Still drinking like a fish, I suppose?"

Fazil smiled thinly.

"I've a bottle of his favourite Russian vodka for him in the cupboard. Don't let me forget to give it to you. In a nice, plain box, of course. I hear you're playing cricket."

"Yes, sir."

"Oh, please. Drop the 'sir'. I'm family to you, Fazil. Call me Salim. So, what do you dream of becoming?"

"Dream?"

"Yes, you're a young man – young enough to have dreams. We all have them, even me. And they don't leave you. It's just that some people don't reach out to them until they're in the grip of a fucking nightmare." He chuckled.

The tea and coffee arrived, and Fazil opted for a cup of sweet, milky Pakistani chai.

"Tell me about your cricket. You're a fast bowler, eh? Top wicket-taker for City this season, yaar?

"You seem to know a lot about me, s … Salim."

"That's my job. Nineteen next month, living in Bharia town. Best friend, Abdul Shakoor Mahsud? Correct?"

Fazil nodded.

"And maybe there are a few things I know about you that you don't even know yourself."

"Such as?" Fazil was beginning to get nervous about the direction the conversation was taking. He could feel the sweat running under his armpits and a prickling on the back of his neck.

"Well, you might like to know that you are on the long list for the tour to Australia this winter."

"How do you know that?"

Salim laughed. "Trust me, I know. And I could easily get you on the plane. Even into the one-day side. Tell me, what do you think of Imran Khan?"

"He was our greatest all-rounder and one of the best captains of Pakistan."

"And now? What do you think of him as a politician?"

"I don't know much about politics, Salim."

"Good answer," said Salim with a thin chuckle. "And did you know that your friend Abdul Shakoor is a supporter of Imran Khan."

"No. And that's his business, not mine."

"Or that his brother Bilal Agha is a fighter for the TTP?"

"Why are you asking me?"

"I could tell you a great deal about the Mehsud family. There are a lot of them in Wazirstan – though not as many as there used to be, thanks to our intelligence and the help of our American friends."

"Abdul is not a terrorist."

"I know. At least not yet anyway. But his bloody family is up to its neck in the damn terrorist game with Daesh and the Taliban."

"You said yourself, it's a big family. Abdul Shakoor doesn't …"

"Listen to me, Fazil. I know a radical when I see one. He talks a lot to you. And I think you're a good listener."

"What are you saying? That I shouldn't be friends with Abdul?"

"On the contrary. I would like you to get to know him even better. Maybe you can both go to Australia. A couple of injuries, and we could fast track you into the Pakistan Test team. What do you think of that?"

Fazil shook his head in disbelief.

"Ha. Your father told me you were a bit naïve. But you'll come round all right. 'Nineteen-year-old quick makes his debut for Pakistan in Perth' – how does that sound to you as a headline? It's up to you if you want to see it in print."

Salim got up from his chair and took Fazil's arm. He raised him gently to his feet. "It's a lot to think about," he said. "We'll have another little chat very soon. Meanwhile, keep this to yourself. Ah, and here's that bottle of vodka for your dear father."

Fazil didn't remember much about the return journey. The same Land Rover took him from the compound to his home, and he sat in the back, head buzzing with questions. Was Abdul Shakoor in danger? Should he tell him what Salim Malik had said? Or would that place him in greater danger? Why did Salim want him to spy on Abdul? Or was that just the beginning? If he agreed to the deal Salim was offering, to play for Pakistan, what would the next demand be?

When he got home Fazil poured the bottle of vodka down the sink and opened his laptop. There was the offer from Ramsbottom. He quickly ran off an email. *I accept. Please send full contract.* Then he rang Abdul Shakoor.

"We've got to meet. Now. I'll come to your place."

SLIP

SLIP
South Africa

Danny stood in the door of the changing room, A muscular figure, not tall but his powerful physique accentuated by his pads and thigh guard. He held his weighty, long-handled bat in one hand and his gloves and helmet in the other. He was sweating profusely after scoring an aggressive 82 which had practically steered the team to victory in the De Beers Cup semis. With 15 overs to go, they needed just 26 runs to qualify for the final of the trophy for the first time in the club's history.

"Well batted, mate," said Wolf, looking up briefly from putting on his own pads. He was next in. But the expression on Danny's face stopped him in his tracks – he knew.

Danny and Wolf had been friends for 20 years, ever since Wolf started playing for St George's colts. It was less than a year after Mandela became president, and the country was undergoing massive change. Danny became only the second black player to play for the first team. Wolf recalled that initial morning in the nets. Danny was a natural, strong and quick on his feet, fearless when facing the short, fast stuff.

He and Wolf had hit it off from the moment they first played together, They were an unusual pairing in those days: the stocky, Xhosa opening bat and the tall, willowy, fair-haired Afrikaner all-rounder.

Playing for the same team from the age of 14 shaped their teenage years. Danny forced his way into the first XI a whole season before Wolf. But Wolf's slow left-arm bowling took him to the top of the averages the following year. They were friends in competition, and such was their obsession with the game that they often found themselves isolated, even from their cricket-loving peers, by their endless talk of team selection, tactics, pitch conditions and cricketing history.

Their friendship took them to the heart of each other's family. Wolf loved eating and Danny's Ma was a wonderful cook who revealed to him the pleasures of lamb stew and umngqusho with sugar beans, butter and potatoes. They went on holiday together, to the Cape. And, when they weren't playing cricket, they played guitar or swam at Blue Horizon Bay or hung out at school.

Today's game for St George's was a crucial cup semi-final clash with league leaders Heatherbank. The home side was lingering at around halfway in the league after an up-and-down season, and the Cup was their only realistic chance of a trophy this year. After winning the toss St George's had caught Heatherbank on the hop, inserting them on a drying pitch.

Early wickets from the seamers had put the break on the scoring rate. Then the spinners came on and more wickets fell. Wolf had been pleased with his spell. It felt, to quote his coach, that he'd put a shoe box on a length and could hit it at will. He'd taken only two wickets but, with an economy rate of under three an over, he'd racked up the pressure on the opposition batters, which had brought wickets for the bowlers at the other end. Heatherbank were finally dismissed for 195, with three of their fifty overs remaining.

As they walked off, Danny jogged up to his best friend grinning happily. "Great bowling, mate," he said, giving

Wolf a mighty hug. "50 short of a par score. It's ours to lose."

Aged 18, Wolf went on to study sports technology at Wits University. Danny got a job as a salesman with his uncle's agricultural equipment business. And for three years they saw each other only in the university vacations. Danny continued to pile up the runs for St George's where he established himself as a free-scoring opening bat, while Wolf played erratically for the university seconds as a useful all-rounder, batting at seven or eight and adding a home-made doosra to his left-arm-spin repertoire.

Their friendship would probably have drifted had Wolf moved away after uni, which had been on the cards. He'd considered a spell in Europe but, in his third year at Wits, he married Debra, a popular and pretty girl from Durban, who was studying medicine and represented the university as a long-jumper. They planned to have children as soon as she qualified as a doctor, and to move to Cape Town, but she got posted to the Livingstone Hospital and they settled in Port Elizabeth where, to pay the mortgage, Wolf took a job as a PE teacher in a local school. He immediately regained his place in St George's first team.

Those were the golden years of their friendship. Danny was working as a sales director for his uncle's company and earning good money. They went to restaurants and concerts together and dusted down their guitars and played at Wolf's flat over a few beers when Debra was working nights. But mostly it was cricket. They topped the batting and bowling averages respectively for two consecutive seasons, and Wolf scored his first century for the club in a 200-plus-run partnership with Danny.

Wolf was Danny's best man when he married Farai. He had only met her once before the wedding – as Danny joked, "'You don't want every good-looking bloke in the neighbourhood ogling up your wife before you're safely married."

Farai had been living in Jo'burg and training as a physiotherapist before she met Danny but it was, in a sense, a traditional Xhosa marriage – arranged by the two families, who came from the same village. Of course, the couple were given plenty of leeway to get to know each other and veto the plans if they wanted to. And, though the marriage took them back to their roots, neither of them now saw much of their old family homes, returning perhaps once a year to see their grandparents.

Farai's beauty was the talk of the cricket club. The wedding reception was held in the St George's pavilion, and all the players and members were invited. Two oxen were roasted in the traditional manner, and there was dancing through the night to Xhosa bands with their vibrant, infectious beat and rhythm. In the early hours Farai, encouraged by Danny, asked Wolf to dance and he looked into her eyes ...and how he wished he hadn't.

There was no suppressing that look or the memory of her. It was reinforced every time they met: a glance that lingered, a knowing smile. There were frequent meals and picnics and Debra and Farai became good at organising things around work and cricket matches and they, too, became close friends. Farai did a further physiotherapy course at the Livingstone, specialising in sports injuries, doing some freelance work for the club, which resulted in the inevitable ribald comments from some of the less enlightened players, though never in front of Danny.

One afternoon a few months later Wolf had arranged to drop round some cricket kit for Danny. When he arrived at the flat, Farai told him Danny had been called away suddenly to sort out a problem with an important client's new combine harvester. She asked him in for a drink. He mentioned his sore bowling shoulder. She gave him a massage. And, after the passion, the mouth of hell opened before them and swallowed them up.

It was during tea between innings that Wolf's crumbling world finally fell apart. One of the players' wives, sitting next to Danny, took it upon herself to tell him all the rumours that were flying about concerning his wife and his best friend. Danny dismissed it all as malicious gossip, but after tea he began to think about it further. The stories he had heard were, of course, ridiculous … but something about them nevertheless appeared to tally with events as he remembered them.

By the time he walked out to open the innings for St George's, he was confused and angry. In cricketing terms, his fellow opener Seth O'Brien was his diametrical opposite in every respect. Tall, angular and elegant, Seth was a natural defensive player who adapted to the 50-over game by playing the angles. Danny was an out-and-out attacker, fluent, quick on his feet and he hit the ball hard with a mighty follow-through. Today, though, he stepped up the aggression to another level. He seemed intent on grinding the opposition into the earth.

Early in his innings, after Danny swung heartily and missed an out-swinger, the keeper thought the time was ripe for a little light sledging. "You're out of your class, feller. Why not pack up and go home to the missus."

"Talk about my wife again, and this goes up your arse," said Danny, brandishing his bat.

The next three balls went four, six, four.

For several days after the fateful afternoon, Wolf avoided Farai's and Danny's company. The agony of betraying both Debra and his best friend was overwhelming. Of course, he told himself it was a one-off. Never to be repeated.

The repeat came ten days later, their desire overwhelming everything else in their lives. At first, they talked about it as if it hadn't really happened. She said things like, when we go back to real life. But she also said ... if only this could be our real life.

The guilt came in waves, for both of them: over the months Wolf lost count of the number of times that Farai told him it was over. But they always returned, locked together in love and guilt. Even when he was away from her he could hear her laughter, see the dreamy look in her eyes or the expression that told him she was teasing him. He was haunted by the smell of her body after sex, he dreamed of the flatness of her belly. And, when they came together again, he could scarcely believe that the shudder that ran through her body as he embraced her was a response to his close presence. She was a mystery and a magnet for him. And he no longer understood his own being; his reactions, his passion, his madness were all alien to him.

As the weeks passed he felt himself caught up in something unknowable and frightening, and he had no compass for navigating the course of his life. Where would this lead them? Living in fear and excitement at the risk they were taking.

Amidst the maelstrom of lies there were moments of panic and sometimes absurdity. He remembered one conversation with Farai, after they had made love in a cheap motel on the far side of town.

I started telling Danny last night, said Farai.

About us?

Yes, well, sort of … I was half crazy. I had this mad urge to confess. For a moment I thought he might understand and forgive us. It was weird because I know that if he ever finds out he will kill you … and me too, probably.

What did you say?

I told him that I thought you fancied me. I said you were a good-looking guy. And then I saw the look in his eyes, and I said I guess that makes two of us in love with Wolf. Only I understood that he had the first call on you because he's known you all his life and he's more into white guys than me.

And what did he say?

He laughed.

There were times when Wolf thought the race thing was part of the reason he felt out of his depth. All the years he'd known Danny he'd never discussed it or thought about it much, though there were always people, still infused with the DNA of apartheid, who would mock the strong friendship that had grown up between the two boys. But his love of Farai, confused by its forbiddenness and its intensity, was easy prey to doubts. What did he know of black women? Like most white South Africans he felt he knew plenty about the Xhosa culture, but now his understanding was beginning to appear superficial. He was losing his bearings.

And then the rumours started and the innuendoes. The wife of the team's wicket-keeper had seen them together in a hotel lobby. For weeks Wolf felt an edginess around his team-mates and once or twice, after a few drinks had been taken, there were cruder comments intended for Wolf's hearing. But no-one, of course, told Danny.

And then, three weeks ago, Debra had announced, in a matter of fact sort of way, that she was pregnant. Wolf was so *completely taken aback that he asked her to repeat what she had said. They hadn't had sex for months … except for that once on holiday in Cape Town. When he told Farai he saw that it was a watershed for her.*

"That's it," she said. "We stop. Now."

And for three whole weeks they hadn't seen each other. The craving hadn't gone away but Wolf knew his life had to change. He needed to restore some faith in himself, and he was ashamed, too, that he hadn't taken the initiative in ending the affair.

The heads of the fielding side had gone down long before Danny's explosive innings came to an end. He holed out at long-on going for his fifth six. As soon as he'd left the pitch he rang Farai. Her hesitant answer to his question left him in no doubt.

Wolf looked up into the eyes of his friend. He didn't attempt to move or defend himself. The heavy bat descended in an arc. Edge on, it would strike him, shattering the lower frontal bone of the cranium immediately above his right eye, and sink into the soft tissue of his cerebral cortex. He fancied he heard gasps around him, a cry – it might have been his own. And then blackness …

EDGE

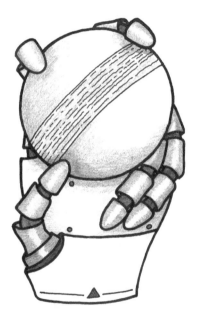

EDGE
U.A.E.

Dubai International Cricket Stadium 2029

Song Li took a step to meet the ball. He felt the tug of his *roBoot,* positioning his left foot perfectly for the cover drive with a split-second correction for the late out-swing. His *Kookaburra K2* described a smooth arc, aligned by the tracker signal from his *Sony Cricvisor.* The ball flew off the face of the bat and powered into the side netting – *152kph ball speed; 96.4% contact* flashed across the top of the visor screen.

The latest intelligent practice aids – from *interior ergonomics* to *personal sensor trackers* were all designed to develop muscle memory. After three net sessions with *roBoot,* the makers claimed, you were primed to move into positions naturally out in the middle. It got your feet going early in the innings when most batters were rooted to the spot.

Song Li, the first Chinese-born global cricket star, was in Dubai to represent and captain a World Champions XI in the most publicised game of international cricket in living memory. Song would bat at three in a team made up of all the greats in world cricket. It included England all-rounder, Rajab Ali the highest paid cricketer ever, Tibor MacLane the USA quick who was bowling consistently at 160 kph, and the great spinning genius from Afghanistan Anwar Sajid Khan. They were all in Dubai … and here for the money.

The game – a one-off T20 day-nighter – was billed 'the Billion Dollar Challenge'. A cool $1billion – winner takes all, put up by the broadcasters, Star-Fox and the Crown Prince of the Emirates, Sheik Faisal Hussein. Many had also dubbed it 'the death of cricket', but there was no doubt that the promoters had found a formula that had, for once, got the whole world talking about cricket instead of football. Whereas an ODI at the International Cricket Stadium between India and Pakistan would normally play to a three-quarters-empty arena, all the tickets for this game had been snapped up within 15 minutes of going online. And the main talking point was not the money or the star quality of the World XI … but the other team. Because the challenge came from a team of robots.

The Cricbots XI had developed – almost inevitably – out of the technological advances that brought such great changes to the game in the first two decades of the 21st century. Indeed, some of the old brands still lingered on in the names of the Cricbot star performers: Hawk-Eye the demon swing bowler and final-over yorker specialist and Two-Step Snicko, the leg-spinner.

The odds being offered by the world's bookmakers and the fixers of the dark internet fluctuated hourly in the feverish environment that preceded the game. But the Cricbots were consistently clear favourites, even though the rules of the game placed strong restrictions on their performance. It had been decided by the game's promoters – with the usual limp acceptance from the ICC – that fast bowling speeds should be limited to 160 kph, and the bat swing coefficients of the robots would be regulated to create a level playing field with their human counterparts.

The broadcast and print media, whilst relishing the spectacle and extracting every last thimbleful of salacious juice out of the story, were at the same time universally critical. In the extremely likely event that the robots won, they claimed, the game of cricket would be side-lined to a sporting irrelevance. Their online opponents countered with the argument that people play chess with robots, they take robots out to dinner, they have sex with robots and they can hire a robot for any conversation under the sun, from the history of philosophy to the future of entertainment and partying. So why, they argued, couldn't you play cricket with a team of robots?

The game had changed so much in the past two decades that it was now considered utterly fruitless to argue against the innovators. The ICC from its Dubai headquarters had presided over the death of Test match cricket, apart from a biennial Ashes series, and the total disappearance of the English County Championship after 140 years of tradition. Television rights had an even tighter stranglehold on the cricket calendar and, as usual, the World Robo Final, as it was being marketed, was free to view everywhere except in countries where there was a large concentration of cricket fans.

In spite of the heat the stadium was full by two in the afternoon – a full three hours before the action was due to begin. The audience was being entertained by a concert featuring international mega star Ho Li Fuk and the celebrity band Big Ossian. The $1 billion prize money and the high price of seats in the shade had flushed out all the oil sheikhs in the region as well as tycoons, bankers, pop stars, actors, heads of state, warlords and gangsters from all over the world. Flights from India had been fully booked for over a month. Men and women who had never attended a cricket match in their lives had hurriedly mugged up on the basic laws of the game and were prominently in attendance in all their finery. It surpassed the Olympics or the football World Cup Final as the must-be-seen-at event of the decade.

The Cricbots XI won the toss – it was, curiously, the one thing the robot team couldn't do for themselves, so it was left to their mortal team manager, ex-global cricket star and broadcaster Joe Root, to call "heads" – and unsurprisingly he chose to bat.

The umpires took the field and, to ear-splitting applause and an interminable drum roll, Song Li led out the World Champions. Each player was announced to the crowd to a fanfare of individually chosen music, which delayed the start of the game by a further 15 minutes.

Then, as if to prove that robots don't conform to a single model, the two specialist openers emerged from the pavilion. The Little Master was short and squat, and he ran out on rotating short legs. Towering above him came WG2, nearly two metres tall with long levers and a spring in his step. The difference in height was partly designed to add to the problems of the bowling attack: a length ball to WG2 was a long hop to the Little Master.

WG2 got them off the mark with a four, carved backward of point. The bat sounded ultra sweet and there were gasps from the crowd at the speed that the ball travelled over the outfield and leapt high in the air as it hit the boundary board.

In the run-up to the game, most of the on-line cricket commentators were of the view that technology was now so good it would be nigh impossible to find any flaws in Cricbots' top order batting. They were programmed to pick the ball from the hand and read the rotation or degree of swing in the air. But the new generation of machines now had built-in evolutionary learning technology using algorithms to learn quickly from any mistake. This meant that the skills of bowlers in developing their repertoire was constantly being overtaken by the batter's response.

There was appreciative applause from the crowd when Tibor MacLane's slingy pace surprised the Little Master in his first over and the late away swing took the ball past the edge of the bat. But the next, almost identical delivery saw the robot, stepping a little further across and driving on the up to the boundary.

The two openers put on a partnership of 50 chanceless runs, at over ten an over, but then WG2 hooked a shortish delivery in the air backward of square. It looked a certain six until the ball held up in the stiff breeze and Rajab Ali, scampering round the boundary, took a perfectly judged one-handed catch and managed to keep his feet just inside the laser rope.

In came the much vaunted 10KO6. 10KO1 had been the very first of the robot batters, launched in 2020. According to its Indian manufacturers it featured the combined super-human characteristics of Sachin Tendulkar and Virat Kolhi. The latest model was said to be invincible against any bowling.

Li turned to his spinners. As usual there was a bit of turn in the UEA pitch, albeit on the slow side. But 10KO was up to the challenge. Anwar Sajid's first over went for 4,2,4,2,2,6 and the straight six off the flipper flew way over the sight screen to Anwar's obvious despair and disbelief.

At the halfway point of the innings the score was 128 for one and, as the momentum built, the Robos looked unstoppable. But hubris was to be their downfall. The Little Master clipped a dipping low full-toss on the on-side and called for a run. 10KO set off and then barked, 'No'. The opener's legs went into reverse, its feet slipped a little before the dive, and the direct throw from square-leg beat the robot to the line by two centimetres. 'OUT' flashed up on all the ad-boards around the ground, even before the umpire could raise her finger.

Robot No 4 was The Blaster who took batting to its most destructive. It arrived in the middle to the theme tune from last year's blockbuster movie, '13 Minutes to Oblivion'. Thirteen minutes of The Blaster and it would be game over. Three consecutive sixes flowed off the bat, brutally struck straight, heaved over square-leg and ramped over the keeper. Things were looking bleak for Song Li's team, but then The Blaster proved that even robots can suffer from over-confidence. It went down the track to a well-disguised slower ball which veered past pads and flailing bat. Blaster turned to see the keeper holding the ball in his gloved fist and grinning at his adversary as he casually lifted off the bail.

"Lovely work, Dessie," shouted Rajab Ali, enveloping the little keeper in a bear hug. It was a big wicket, and all the team knew it as they gathered round to congratulate both bowler and keeper.

170 for three with five overs left. 10KO was calling the shots but the World XI's fielding was breathtaking. Twos were reduced to singles and boundaries cut off with acrobatic dives.10KO saw rather less of the strike than was ideal, and the pressure began to mount a little. Another run-out showed that there was still work to be done on robotic calling between the wickets. 10KO responded by taking 18 off an over from Anwar Sajid. But Rajab Ali came back and blasted out the robo-all-rounder 2Brain

with a reverse swinging yorker that would have cleaned up any batter in the world. The Cricbots finished on 246, a massive mountain to climb on a slow, turning pitch. But perhaps not as bad as it might have been, and morale was reasonably high as Song Li led his team off the field.

The floodlights lit up the stadium as highlights of the innings were screened around the ground, accompanied by thunderous music and a robotic dance performance by the 100 stars of the musical '2084'.

Song Li was at the crease sooner than he might have wished; the first wicket fell with the fourth ball of Hawk-Eye's opening over – a short, rearing bouncer and the unsuspecting South African opener Henok Howard ducked but failed to get his bat out of the way. Stumpy, the keeper, ran back and took the catch over its shoulder.

Li took his time. He waited for the fielders to move their positions and surveyed the gaps. As he did so Stumpy stepped forward from behind the stumps.

"Hey, skipper," drawled the machine in west-coast robotic. "Any chance that uncle of yours could fix me up with a loan?"

Someone had been doing their homework on the sledging front. It wasn't widely known that Li's father's younger brother, a director of China Bank, had just been imprisoned for fraud. Or that Li was particularly fond of Uncle Wei.

"I doubt a tin box would have the credit rating," said Li, calmly tapping the crease and then taking his guard.

He could have perished from the first four balls he received. First off Hawk-Eye served up a ripper. It pitched on middle and off, angling into the right-hander, then went screaming past the outside edge. Li was probably the best batsman in the world, but he considered himself lucky to have missed it rather than edging to the keeper.

Then he was dropped in the slips, or would have been if anyone other than the Little Master had been standing there; its desperate leap failed to get a touch on the ball and they ran two. The third delivery swung in and somehow he got the benefit of the doubt for lbw – the review showed 'umpire's call', clipping off stump. Another in-nipper passed a hair breadth over middle stump. A lesser batsman would have thrown in the towel, but Li had that stamp of greatness in his ability to put the might-have-beens out of his head and keep his mind fresh.

Hawk-Eye was rested after the one over, but Paceman and Speedo kept up the pressure, making batting very difficult with swing, seam and change of pace. The batters played out two maidens before back-to-back boundaries got the scoreboard moving at last. Li had never batted before with Archie Slim, the Australian captain, but he'd played against him on many an occasion. Archie's ODI average of 61.3 was surpassed only by Li himself amongst current players.

Two-Step Snicko took over at the Royal Box end after the power play, with a repertoire of leg-breaks, googlies and top spinners. Slim was lucky to survive a reverse sweep, which was top-edged just over the fielder positioned halfway to the boundary for the catch.

As the eighth over ended, Li knew the game was rapidly running away from them; the required run rate was now nearly 15 an over. They needed to raise the risk stakes.

He and Archie discussed tactics, and Archie opted to take the long handle to the spinner. He carved two sixes over mid-wicket before being spectacularly caught by

2Brain on the cover boundary. In came Rajab Ali, pushed up the order to give the scoring rate some much needed momentum.

At the halfway mark they were 99 for two and well off the pace. Rajab struck two more boundaries before holing out at long-off. And then disaster. Two wickets in two balls gave Snicko a hat-trick, and the World XI was looking down the barrel of a blunderbuss at 110 for five.

Yet another new game plan was needed, and Li told the incoming bat, wicket-keeper Desmond Kani, to push the singles while he took responsibility for the boundaries. That was no easy task with 2Brain taking the pace off the ball. But Paceman returned for an over, and Li used his speed off the pitch to squeeze three boundaries through the ring. With five overs to go they needed 88 to win. Mission impossible.

Li made it known that he was going down fighting. He had the crowd on its feet with a towering straight six, followed by a ramped four which bounced once and flew over the laser rope. Another six followed before the pendulum swung again. Kani edged a simple catch to the keeper, and Stumpy set off on a lap of honour.

Snicko came on to bowl its final over, and Li decided he had no choice but to target the canny little spinner-robot. A massive six flew onto the Robo's changing room balcony and was caught by Joe Root. Another fell just short of the Royal Box. But soon the seventh wicket went down to an athletic caught-and-bowled. With two overs remaining they required 41 runs – the scoreboard read 206 for seven.

Li and the new batter, Anwar Sajid, met in the middle of the pitch.

"One more for the century, skip," said Anwar.

Li hadn't even noticed. "I'll celebrate when we win," he said. And then with a smile he added, "Swing hard for the human race."

Anwar missed Speedo's first delivery which screamed through just over his bails. But he connected with the second and cleared the cover boundary. A single brought Li on strike. A perfect cover drive streaked across the boundary. His century was celebrated by the crowd and his team mates on the balcony but not by the batter himself; Li just raised his bat once and got on with his work, always with an eye on the scoreboard. Two more boundaries – and with an over to go they needed 22 to win.

"Get something on it and run," said Li to Anwar, knowing that their only hope now lay in his grabbing the strike. Hawk-Eye was the death bowler, and the field was set for the robot's specialist in-swinging yorkers.

But the roar of the crowd and thrill of the moment was too much for Anwar. He took a mighty swing at the fully pitched ball honing in on his stumps and got an edge past the keeper … all the way to the boundary. Li glared at him and he avoided eye contact. The next yorker was faster still and he was down the wicket. The ball skewed off his pad and he ran. Hawk-Eye, still appealing for the lbw, picked up and threw at the stumps. A direct hit, but Li was in and screamed 'No' to Anwar who wanted the overthrow as the ball ricocheted away.

The Robos called for a review for the lbw but were told they were out of time by the umpire. There was a bit of robo-grumbling and kicking of the turf, but finally they all returned to their fielding positions.

17 needed from four balls. Hawk-Eye charged in. The yorker was inch perfect but Li had gone down the track and ramped it on the full over the keeper's outstretched glove for another four. The next was a slow bouncer. Li was almost beaten by the pace but guided it down to long leg for two runs. 11 needed. Two balls remaining.

Hawk-Eye fired in yet another inch-perfect yorker, but Li shimmied down the pitch and hit the ball on the full clean over long-on for six. The crowd was chanting, 'Li Song, Li Song!' He eyed the field again. The long-on and long-off brought into the circle. He expected a short ball. Four to tie, six to win. It was a double bluff. Hawk-Eye's yorker was blisteringly fast. Li swung too late and he heard the death rattle of his timbers as he followed through. Game over.

There was a silence around the ground and in the middle the Robots began their celebrations. Hawk-Eye was picked up by WG2 and hoisted onto 10KO's shoulders.

But what was happening? The umpires were conferring. Had the bowler overstepped? No. But in the heat of the moment Hawk-Eye had wound up the pace. 164kph. No ball … exceeding the speed limit. The umpire signalled – free hit. Now four to win

A roar went round the stadium as the crowd finally realised what was happening. Hawk-Eye was back at his mark and tearing at the turf with its feet. The crowd began to clap as Hawk-Eye again ran in. Short of a length and Li pulled. Square leg dived and missed. 2Brain jetted around the boundary from mid-wicket, putting in a despairing dive but deflecting the ball along the laser rope … now scrambling to recover it, but the ball gently touched the boundary and the screens around the ground simultaneously signalled FOUR. Li raised his bat to the sky.

They had won! Stumpy patted him on the back. For all the sledging Stumpy was a sporting robot after all. Hawk-Eye slumped to its robotic knees.

SPIN

SPIN
Sri Lanka

His mother had always been the driving force behind his ambitions as a young cricketer. *Am'ma* was a Tamil from Trincomalee. All her family were crazy about the game, but she was without equal in her fanaticism. She worshipped the Sri Lankan team day and night. And of all her heroes, one stood out head and shoulders above the rest. *Murali.*

As a child Adam felt he knew Muttiah Muralitharan better than he knew his dad. Not that he'd ever met Murali, but scarcely a day went by without him hearing a reference to the great man. *Eat up your daal, it's Murali's favourite food. Murali likes milk chocolate so it can't be bad for you. You'd never hear Murali speak like that.*

Adam was born to be a spin bowler. He was a left-armer and, though his mother tried for a long time to persuade him to bowl right-arm like Murali, she eventually gave up. With his distinctive long-arm action and supple wrists, by his early teens he had mastered the doosra and a top-spin variation as well as a perfectly disguised arm ball. He spent hours bowling taped tennis balls against the side wall of their house in Grandpass, perfecting his action, inventing variations of loop and flight which were so essential on the slow Colombo wickets. Am'ma coached him every day. She was unrelenting in her quest for perfection and would punish him severely with loss of privileges if she felt he wasn't trying a hundred percent.

When Adam started playing club cricket at the age of 15 – not for Tamil Union, Murali's old club, as his mother had hoped, but for Colombo Colts – the coaches and other players all assumed he came from a single-parent family. His mother was a constant presence at the club, but his father never once put in an appearance and Adam didn't talk about him at all.

His dad was from a Christian family from Negombo, though he hadn't been inside a church for years and his people had turned their back on him when he'd married a Tamil. He'd been a truck driver when Adam was young – always away from home. But serious back problems put paid to his driving, and after that his life began to unravel. Now he did a few part-time jobs for cash, but he was at home most of the time, bad-tempered, surly, often drunk.

Very few young players in Colombo had come up against a bowler like Adam. Most of them had been 'properly' coached at the top private schools such as St Thomas' College, Royal and Trinity. There were some fine young batters playing for Colts' Under-17s; Madushan Perera and Kavinda Jayakody were both tipped for a future with the national team, but in the nets Adam consistently tormented and bamboozled his team-mates.

Whilst his bowling skills may have initially ruffled a few feathers and caused some resentment towards the young left-arm spinner, Adam's performances in club competitions soon raised him to hero status. In his first season with the U17s he was the top wicket-taker and took four five-fors.

But even after playing for Colts for over a year, Adam remained an outsider. The privileged background of most of the team members meant that their conversations about tennis parties and weekends at Galle and game fishing at Kirinda always left Adam out in the cold. He was only on their wavelength when the talk returned to cricket, which fortunately was relatively frequently.

Nevertheless, he enjoyed listening to the other boys talking, especially Madushan. Madushan 'Mad' Perera was the son of a leading Colombo barrister, who lived near the coast in the most expensive part of Colombo 07 district. Mad was tall and slim with startling blue eyes and a regal presence which made him a natural choice for team captain. He batted with confidence, amounting almost to disdain of the opposition's bowling attack. Am'ma thought he was arrogant – what she said was, *that boy thinks he's the centre of the damn universe* – but in Adam's eyes Mad could do no wrong.

The final game of the season was the Singer Cup final against Nondescripts. Colts won the toss and Madushan's century in even time ensured that they posted a challenging score of 311 for six on a slow wicket and a damp outfield. Nondescripts' chase began promisingly and then became bogged down against the slower bowlers. The game seemed set up for Adam when the captain brought him on at 125 for four.

His first over, a succession of wides and long hops went for 17 runs. The second yielded another 14 and Mad took him off.

"You got a problem, Adam?" asked the skipper.

Adam shook his head, but he knew the ball wasn't coming out right. He felt heavy-limbed, as if he was sickening for a cold, perhaps.

"Well, maybe I'll bring you back in a couple of overs," said Mad. "Keep yourself loose."

Nondescripts took advantage of the mid-innings impetus and put on another 40 runs for the fifth wicket before a run-out ended the partnership. At 207 for five with the game in the balance, Mad brought Adam back into the attack. His first ball was cracked back over his head for six and two wides down the leg side followed. Adam felt his brain scrambling – he didn't have a plan because he'd never been in this sort of situation before, never felt so totally out of control.

Mad came over and put an arm around his shoulder. Adam felt his knees give way slightly as the captain spoke firmly but calmly into his ear. "Take a deep breath and think what you're going to bowl. You've got the skills to see this lot off. We're counting on you, Adam."

The next ball was the first he'd landed on a length and it fizzed past the right-hander's outside edge. Mad gave him an encouraging look and a thumbs up. The next took the same line and the batter played and missed again. Doosra next, decided Adam. He pitched it on off stump and it spun back into the pads. Plumb lbw. The umpire agreed.

"I knew you could do it," said Mad, arm round his shoulder again and then a ruffle of his hair. Adam grinned, a warm feeling of pleasure rose within him and his face burned.

Now he was on a roll. The new batter lasted two balls, clean bowled by the top-spinner. In his next over the arm ball, cleverly flighted, brought him his third wicket, caught behind, and a sharp caught-and-bowled reduced their opponents to 238 for nine. It was all over. Ravi, the opening bowler, wrapped it up.

Soon they were back in the changing room, celebrating and reliving the highlights of their victory. Madushan was voted man of the match, but Adam's four-wicket haul had won them the game. The trophy on the table had already been photographed many times in everyone's hands, including Adam's.

"Party tonight at my place," announced Madushan. "You're all invited. Bring anyone you like. We've got the place to ourselves – my folks are away for the weekend."

"You coming?" Ravi asked Adam.

"How am I going to get there?" said Adam.

"My brother'll pick you up."

"Not sure," said Adam. He knew what his mother would say. But if ever there was a party he wanted to go to, this was it.

In the end he got his way. Am'ma wasn't happy, particularly when he told her it was at Madushan's place. But he persuaded her that, since it was the last game of the season, he needed to celebrate the victory with his friends.

"Home by 1 o'clock latest," she said. "And no drinking."

Adam thought that was a bit unnecessary. He'd never touched a drop of alcohol in his life. But he promised all the same.

Ravi's brother drove them through the security gates of the Perera mansion, between lawns that sparkled green in the floodlights. A thud of amplified bass grew louder as they approached the magnificent house, a white colonial-style residence encircled with verandahs and balconies.

"Aya! I knew that Mad's old man was loaded, but this is something else," said Ravi.

"Hope the food's in the same class," said Ravi's brother who was distinctly on the paunchy side.

Madushan greeted them as they entered the house through a grand glass-walled vestibule. He was dressed in a white shirt and very tight jeans, and he seemed to be enjoying his role of getting the party off to a swing. Adam couldn't take his eyes off him.

Soon they were standing around in groups in a large salon full of tall palms and other tropical plants. A small army of waiters got up in white uniforms and bright blue turbans was plying the guests with drinks and what Ravi's brother called canapés – and he took two huge handfuls of them each time a tray came past.

Adam held a fresh orange juice in his hand and was listening over the beat of the music to the conversation of a group of his team-mates about their chances of getting into the Under-19s next season. The music got a little louder, interspersed with some jokey banter from the DJ, and the general hubbub intensified as more guests arrived. Apart from the Colts players and a couple of their girlfriends, Adam knew absolutely no one. There were almost as many girls in the gathering as boys. Everyone was very expensively dressed, and Adam looked down at his crumpled 'best' trousers and slightly stained trainers with a stab of shame. But his mother's words came to his aid, *Murali is never ashamed of his background. He talks to everyone, beggar or prime minister.*

As his colleagues moved on to get more drinks or talk to friends, Adam found himself standing on his own. He watched the new arrivals being greeted by Mad for a time, and then he walked out through the french windows onto the verandah to get some air. A girl, whom he seemed at first glance to recognise, was sitting in a rattan chair smoking and looking out over the lawns. He then remembered that Madushan had a twin sister. The resemblance was remarkable. He must have stared at her for a moment too long.

"Is there something I can do for you, or are you just quietly admiring my body?" she said.

"Sorry," stammered Adam.

"And who are you?"

In spite of his confusion he managed to tell her his name and that he played cricket with her brother.

"And where do you live, Adam the spin bowler?"

"Grandpass."

"Really! How interesting. Well you can call me Eve, just for tonight. Would you like a drink, Adam?"

She waved at a passing waiter and inspected the tray of drinks.

"Oh perfect, *Snakebite*. The wicked serpent in the Garden."

She took two glasses and handed one to Adam.

"Cheers."

"I don't drink."

"Of course you do, Adam. All Madi's friends drink. Down in one, now. One, two, three."

Out of politeness to Madushan's sister, he drank the cocktail and was surprised by its sweetness. That was followed by a burning sensation in the back of his throat which wasn't altogether unpleasant.

"Good boy. Now one more little Snakebite, and Adam and Eve'll go and see if they can find an apple tree in the Garden of Eden."

She grabbed two more glasses from the waiter and, taking Adam by the hand, she dragged him onto the lawn and into a little grove of fruit trees over to the right-hand side. For the first time Adam realised that she was rather drunk. The warmth of the evening and the cocktail had blunted his own senses, and he allowed himself to be led in a dream-like fashion amongst the trees. They sipped their drinks. The Snakebite didn't seem to him to taste very alcoholic, but in truth he had no idea what 'alcoholic' tasted like, and his cheeks were feeling warmer.

"Ah, Adam," she sighed and suddenly she was kissing him full on the mouth, and her hand was against his stomach and sliding lower.

A blind panic came over him. He didn't want it and he pushed her away, gently at first, then with more force until she suddenly lurched backwards, stumbled and looked up at him. A twisted look of disdain flickered across her face.

"Oh, come now, don't play hard to get. Even Christian boys called Adam are allowed a little fun."

She came at him again, arms around his neck, and her lips felt as though they were going to swallow him up.

"No," he shouted, struggling to free himself.

"What's this?" She spat out the word inches from his face. "Not good enough for you, slum boy? You don't like my kisses." She backed away from him with a dismissive wave of her arm. "Oh, are you going to regret this!" she said. And turning on her high heels she marched unsteadily towards the house.

Adam stood for a moment, trying to grasp the situation through a growing feeling of unease. His head was reeling from the drink and the confusion of the moment. He'd never been kissed by a girl before. Kissed by someone who looked so like Madushan but a girl … he closed his eyes and felt the tears well up. And when he opened them again there Mad was coming towards him. Adam wiped the tears away, trying to focus. There were four of them: Mad in front, Kavinda, he didn't know the other two. He smiled.

"What are you grinning at, you pervert?" screamed Mad, pushing him hard in the chest.

"But I …"

"Think you can come to my fucking house and abuse my sister, eh? What d'you low-life Tamils call it? Eve teasing, isn't it? You disgust me."

"I … I didn't touch her."

"Didn't touch her, eh? Didn't grab her breasts? Didn't try to force yourself on her – here in our gardens?

"No!"

"Well, well. You know what? I believe her. And I don't fucking believe you. Get out of my house before I beat the shit out of you." He gave Adam another fierce shove in the chest, almost knocking him off his feet.

A hard, solid lump had formed under his ribs; it was burning, throbbing as if trying to burst forth out of his chest. He looked into Madushan's eyes and saw only hatred. A cry of anger broke from his mouth, and his left arm swung up from his waist with all his strength. His fist made contact. Blood flowed instantly from Madushan's nose; it ran across those beautiful lips and dripped onto his shirt. Adam watched in that brief moment of silence as the scarlet stains spread over the pure white cotton.

The blows rained down on him. He bent double, with the pain of a punch to his guts, fell to the ground and then they were kicking him – on his back, head and between his legs. From nowhere two security guards appeared and picked him up, violently, grabbing him under the arms. They dragged him across the lawn to jeers and shouts of abuse from the party guests. And then, above all the cries and confusion, Adam heard Madushan shout …

"You're finished, boy. You'll never play cricket in Colombo again."

The gates opened, and the guards threw him bodily face down onto the gravel road. He lay still for a moment, listening to the dull clunk of the gates closing automatically behind him. He was alone.

At length, Adam rose painfully to his feet. His left knee gave way but he flexed it and managed to raise himself to his full height. What would Murali do now? he thought.

He wiped the blood and dirt from his face and, without looking back at the house, he started walking towards Grandpass.

TWELFTH WOMAN

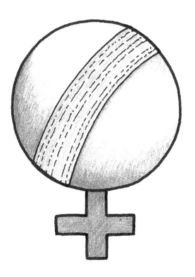

TWELFTH WOMAN

She sensed the moment she woke up that it wasn't going to be a normal day. The sun had risen as usual, light was coming in through the thin blinds, traffic droned and horns sounded in the street, but she knew there had been a shift in the order of things and that today was going to be different.

Poppy her labradoodle, however, didn't appear to recognise the singularity of the day. He greeted her with his boundless enthusiasm, dog lead in mouth, expecting the customary pre-breakfast walk.

"You know what, Pops old boy, I think we'll give it a miss today," she said. He looked at her with his big head tilted to one side and eyes doing special pleading. 'Poppy' had been her father's choice of name because they'd acquired him on Armistice Day and it sounded a bit like puppy. It didn't suit him then, and it was even more ridiculous now that he was a fully grown, shaggy, profoundly randy and disobedient dog. But he answered to the name, and it was too late to change.

"Maybe later, Pops." She relented slightly.

She checked her messages over breakfast. As usual she was alone in the house at this time, late on a Saturday morning. Her father was at work at the shop, and her sister would either be at the gym or the swimming pool, depending on where she and her fitness freak friends had decided to work out today.

And then she saw it. From Tom McCracken, the captain of the First X1.

Hi Helen,
Really sorry about the short notice but we're a
bit short tomorrow. I think we might scrape
eleven but, just in case, could you come along as
12th man. It's a crunch 40-overs game in the
Cup. Get through and we're in the semis. So I
don't want to play with ten men.
Let me know before 11 please.
Tom

Fuckin' nerve, thought Helen. Twelfth man! He can get stuffed. She looked at her watch. Quarter to eleven. She made herself another cup of coffee and read the email again. The fact was that she desperately wanted to play for the first team. And this might be her only chance.

She finished her toast and took a proper look at the weather. It was one of those Leeds days, with the sun half peeping through, when it might rain and it might not. A police car went past with its siren blaring. An old man on the pavement in front of the park gates gave it a V sign. She looked at her watch again. 11.20. I'll call him.

- *Tom?*
- *Yes*
- *It's Helly. What's this about a twelfth woman?*
- *Twelfth woman? Oh I get it. Yeah can you make it?*
- *You reckon I'll get a game?*
- *I dunno. There's a fair chance. Jamie's had 'flu, but he says he'll try and play. Dom's doubtful, too. We're really short, or else I wouldn't ask.*
- *Oh thanks.*
- *Will you?*

- *Guess so. But I can't hang around if there's nowt doing.*
- *Great. See you at 1.30, right?*

Was that the result she wanted? wondered Helen.

The thoughts that then flickered across her brain went something like this: I'm fifteen and I know I'm smart and funny and some people say a bit loud. And dad's always telling me I can be whatever I want to be. I know all this, and I know I'm a good wicketkeeper and quite a good batter and I'm the youngest player in the second XI. But I don't feel a success, particularly when I'm playing with boys because even the nice ones don't really like girls to be funny or clever and they especially don't like them to be as good at sport as they are, and all they talk about – mostly behind my back but not always – is whether I'm FIT or not. Which I am. Not super FIT of course but, even if I don't have the perfect body, it's not bad apart from my bum being too big. And it's none of their business. And anyhow that's not the thing ... if Tom wants a twelfth man and he can't find one and he turns to me as a last resort, what am I supposed to do? Just crawl along and watch them play and say thank you very much for asking me?

Then she thought, if I stand up for myself they'll say you're just whining and making a fuss about nothing. You're over-reacting. Lighten up. That's because they don't want to talk about it, because they don't get it. She could play the bad-ass woman, stand up to them, slog it out. But that wasn't her style. I'll do it my way, she thought, and if they don't like it or don't understand where I'm coming from, tough shit.

She'd told Tom she'd be there and she wasn't going to let him down. Tom was all right. He wasn't one of the brightest, but everyone said he was a good captain – if a bit on the cautious side. At nets he'd helped her with her batting, particularly the short stuff that she'd found quite intimidating to begin with. Now the hook was one of her top shots.

She got the bus to the ground. On the way she read her book – Ali Smith. She loved everything about books, even the way they felt and smelt. But her reading didn't stop her eavesdropping on the conversations around her. There were two young women behind her – she heard them talking and played the game of wondering what they looked like, since she hadn't noticed them when she'd sat down.

- *I went on the pill and put on two stone, right.*
- *That's a pretty effective contraceptive then.*
- *Ha, the funny thing is that I don't see myself as fat.*
- *Aren't people rude to you about it?*
- *Yeah, I get everything from lardy cow to fat bitch, but I just ignore it.*
- *People can be so horrid.*
- *Makes me laugh. What do they think I'm going to say? Fat is beautiful? No, it just happened. What pisses me off is all the new clothes I've had to buy.*

Helen chanced a look over her shoulder avoiding eye contact. One was tall and skinny, the other was a bit fat all right, but she had a sweet face. Asian origin, with head scarves, but perfect Yorkshire accent. Not what she'd expected.

Tom McCracken was the first person she encountered when she walked into the pavilion.

"Thank god you're here. Get your kit on. You're playing. And we're fielding," he said.

There were times when Helen was less than enchanted by the consequences of her decision to play cricket. There was no decent women's team in her area, so she was forced to battle it out for a place with the boys. In the second XI there were two other women who played occasionally, sometimes three when Ellie Baxter was down from uni. But today she'd most likely be the only woman on the park. First, she had to turf the umpires out of their room so that she could get changed, since there were still no proper facilities for women in the pavilion. And then she had not only to prepare her head for the game ahead but also steel herself to handle the macho culture.

"Hello, lass," said Murdo Oxley, the team's fastest bowler. "You making the teas today?"

She yawned. "Sure, Murdo. Teas, cleaning the lav. And I'm going to be multi-tasking as Player of the Match."

It was a tricky balancing act – staying on the line between being 'one of the boys' and dealing with the casual sexism that came her way with tedious regularity. The problem was that it was generally considered ok for a guy to make daft jokes or behave like a feral ten-year old, but girls didn't get the same leeway. If a boy tells a stupid joke he's being a good laugh, but, when a girl does it, it's attention seeking or being a bit weird. As a born joker, Helen wasn't about to suppress her instincts in order to make her team-mates feel more comfortable. She'd put up with the banter to a point but she was quickly on the attack when any of the usual suspects went too far.

She wasn't surprised to find herself fielding at deep square-leg and then deep extra-cover as they changed round at the end of the over. It was hard to feel part of the action as a boundary patroller, but she concentrated hard on what was happening in the middle. Not much, was the long and short of it. The ball wasn't beating the bat but nor were the openers forcing the pace. The run rate plodded along at under three an over until Fergal Gorby, their tall, lanky spinner, came on to bowl.

The third ball of his first over was short, and the batter pulled hard. It was in the air but bounced well short of her and to her right and skimmed off the hard outfield. She ran to cut it off, put in a dive and managed to scoop the ball back before it crossed the rope. She rounded off the performance with a neat throw, one bounce into the keeper's gloves, which earned her a few shouts of encouragement from her team-mates.

The next delivery was quicker, outside off stump. The opener went for a cut and top-edged straight into the keeper's face. He went down clutching his left eye. The bowler, fielders and both umpires gathered around the stricken player.

"You all right, Trev?" asked Fergal. Trev took his bloody hand away from his face and revealed a deep cut under his eye that was pumping blood. The mark of the ball's seam was still imprinted on his cheek.

"Stitches," said one of the umpires. He handed Trev a white cloth to soak up the blood, which was now running down the keeper's shirt.

"Can you take the gloves, Helly?" asked Tom.

"Me?" It came as a complete shock.

"You're a wicket-keeper, aren't you?" He was right, it was the obvious solution to the crisis.

She and Tom stripped Trev of his pads and gloves before he walked off, clutching his head. The pads were a bit big for her and flapped about above her knees. There was a blob of Trev's blood on the left one.

There were two balls left in the over. She crouched low behind the stumps, Tom in the slips gave her an encouraging wink. The batter leaned forward into another forward defensive but the ball nipped in between bat and pad and she took it cleanly just over the top of off stump.

"Lovely bowling," she said to Fergal and, to the batter, "Nice leave."

Tom laughed. "Bit chirpy, aren't you?"

"Can't help it," she said.

The last ball was quicker, the arm ball. The opener went for the drive and it took a thick edge. The ball deflected, hit her right glove and bounced up. She had time to adjust and turned and took it cleanly over her shoulder. "Howzat!"

Her first wicket for the First XI; it felt really good. But she steadied herself amidst the congratulations. Life was a see-saw and she knew it. High in confidence: I can be anything. Low in confidence: they're all better than me. That's why wicket-keeping mattered to her: the pure happiness of hours of working at something and then getting it right. She practised, she concentrated and when it happened – the perfect take – then she knew she had done it on her own. That's why she told her dad, I want to be as good as Sarah Taylor.

Nathan Calloway came on to bowl. Nath fancied himself. He had a nice smile, but he was overweight and a bit of a slob. He bowled little medium-pace cutters off a short run. She stood up to the wicket.

"Nice length, Nath." "Lovely ball, Nath." She encouraged the bowler with every delivery as the remaining opening batsman continued to defend solidly.

Finally the batter turned on her and said, "I'm getting really bored with your commentary, love."

"You're a bit of a connoisseur of boredom, aren't you?" she replied.

"What you mean?"

She shrugged. Two balls later the batter took an uncharacteristic heave at a wide ball and inside-edged straight into his stumps. He gave Helen a black look as he departed.

Tom patted her on the back. "I guess we can put that one down to you and your sledging."

"I didn't know you were so mouthy," said Nathan to her with a grin.

"Rubbish ball, Nath. Always gets the wicket," said Helen.

She knew after those first overs that she was in the zone today. The ball was coming into her gloves with sweet timing and she was moving into position fluidly, instinctively. A diving take down the leg side brought a ripple of applause from her team-mates and the handful of spectators around the boundary.

A third wicket stand of sixty ended with a run-out. She took the throw low down and broke the stumps in one movement, with the batter well out of his ground.

A regular caught behind followed and then a neat stumping and, at 103 for five, she realised proudly that she'd had a hand in every wicket so far.

Their captain reached a chanceless fifty but, next ball, he gloved one down the leg side and she caught it on the dive, appealing in mid-air. The umpire shook his head. There were cries of disbelief from the close fielders.

The following over, the same batter was stone-dead lbw, but again her full-throated appeal was turned down.

"If you don't know the way to the changing room, I can help you," she said to her opponent.

"It were off me bat first," said the batter aggressively.

"Like the one last over?"

He scowled. Perhaps she was going too far. She knew you had to stay on the line between the serious and the playful to tip your opponent off balance. But she couldn't resist it …

"Ah well, third time lucky," she said.

Murdo came back with three wickets at the death, and they were bowled out in the penultimate over for 187, though unfortunately the captain was not out. Tom was pleased.

"Not bad with ten men. We ought to knock that off."

At tea she sat with Tom, Nathan and Fergal. The relief of getting through her first top-ranking game without a dropped catch or even a single fumble buoyed her up. She was so pleased that she even allowed herself to put up with a few patronising comments in silence. Fergal said it was the best display of keeping he'd ever seen from a girl – specially one of her age.

Even Murdo made an attempt at being friendly.

"Sorry about that tea lady bit, lass," he said, as they were queuing up for their sandwiches and cakes. "You kept wicket brilliant."

"That's all right, Murdo. You just need reminding from time to time that you're a higher primate."

"Aye," he said with a puzzled look on his face, followed by a broad grin.

The home side's innings began disastrously. By the end of the fourth over they were 7 for three. Tom and Fergal began the repair job and put on 67 together. Then

Fergal played on, and another two wickets fell almost immediately. At 89 for six it was time to strap on her pads. Trev hadn't returned from the hospital and, even if he did, there was little chance that he would bat. So she was the tenth and last batter.

Tom reached his fifty, and in the same over the hundred came up. He was batting well and positively. Nathan at the other end didn't look so secure, but Tom farmed the strike cleverly and the run rate began to pick up. With eight overs to go they needed 61. Tom carved an enormous six over mid-wicket to boost their hopes, but they were dashed again when Nath lost his off stump.

From then on all eyes were on Tom. He kept them in the game single handedly with a mix of boundaries and singles. She watched every ball nervously, knowing she was next in. 11 came off the 34th over, 12 from the 37th. With two overs to go they needed 18 to win.

Murdo had played sensibly, putting Tom on strike at every opportunity. They'd taken seven runs off the first four balls of the 39th over when Murdo lost his head, swung at a short one and was caught at mid-on.

She walked slowly out to the middle. Tom met her halfway.

"Last ball. Defend it. Don't try and run a single whatever happens," he said.

"Ok."

She took her guard, feeling her hand shaking on the bat handle.

"Watch out, love. He's right quick," said the keeper. "A bit too quick for you."

She watched the bowler run in and deliver. It was short and reared at her off the pitch. She dropped her wrists, pulled her head back and let it hit her on the shoulder. A sharp pain ran down her arm. The ball dropped at her feet.

"Over," shouted the umpire.

"That was brave," said Tom. "You ok?"

"No bother."

"11 off the last over. Here we go."

Concentrate on running, she thought. With luck I won't have to bat again.

The first ball was a perfect yorker which Tom dug out. No run. The second he paddled to fine leg and there was an easy two. The running between the wickets made her feel better. Then Tom upper cut a short one and the ball bounced over the boundary ahead of the diving third-man. Five needed off three balls. Another yorker squirted off Tom's bat down to long-leg. She ran hard. Tom turned for the second.

"No," he screamed. The throw was already on its way. She spun round and grounded her bat behind the crease. She was on strike.

They met in the middle for another conference.

"Take a single," said Tom. "I'll be backing up. Tip and run. Try and knock it into space."

She took her time to look around the field which had moved in to prevent the run.

"Feeling nervous, lass?" said the keeper with a foxy grin.

"No. And you?"

"Nah. Been here before. Bet we win."

"I don't bet. I heard betters always lose."

There was a bit of a gap maybe between square- and short-fine-leg. Not much space on the off-side. The bowler leapt up to the wicket and bowled, short of a length outside off stump. She stepped over, angled her bat, felt the deflection and was off.

The ball travelled quickly along the ground to cover-point's left hand. She ran. Tom had backed up a long way and completed the single almost before she was in full stride. The throw came in to her end, low and fast. She put in a dive as the ball skidded inches past the stumps. A direct hit and she'd have gone. The bowler caught it and broke the stumps. But she was home, sliding through on her stomach. A cheer from the boundary. Now it was all up to Tom. Three needed. Last ball.

Another yorker. But Tom got underneath it. Hammered it straight. She watched it sail over her head as she ran. Tom stopped in mid-pitch, watching the ball bounce over the rope. Gave her a huge hug. They'd won.

The rest of the team rushed out to celebrate with them, and Helen and Tom were hoisted up on shoulders and given a rowdy bounce in front of the pavilion. It wasn't very mature. But that didn't surprise her.

On the bus home she listened in on another conversation. Two elderly blokes this time …

- *They need to get over it, those Remoaners.*
- *Aye. They lost fair and square and it's over.*
- *Why can't they grow up.*
- *That's right. We've had the democratic vote and no-one's listening to them any more. Yet still they go bleating on.*

She turned to face them angrily. About to tell them exactly what she thought of their stupid version of democracy. But they both smiled at her and one of them looked a bit like her grandad and she smiled back.

Then she thought about her day. She'd enjoyed the victory. It was sweet … but it wasn't the main thing.

That was playing the game the best you could. There'd been a glimpse for her of a new world of opportunity – not unconditional but open to those who take their tasks seriously and who understand that shortcuts lead nowhere. Life was confusing and would always be so, but the only way to find your place was to have your own distinct identity, in her case as a woman, a Yorkie, a reader … and maybe as a wicketkeeper.

More cricket fiction by
BOB CATTELL

First XI
Eleven short stories linked by the world of cricket

Glory Gardens
Popular children's series about an unusual cricket team

Butter-Finger
Caribbean cricket trilogy co-written with John Agard

Bowl like the Devil
The ultimate test for a young fast bowler